A SWEET SURRENDER

American Historical Romance

LENA HART

Maroon Ash
PUBLISHING

A SWEET SURRENDER
Copyright © 2015 Lena Hart
2nd Print Edition
Originally published in the *For Love & Liberty* anthology.

ALL RIGHTS RESERVED.

No part of this book may be reproduced or transmitted in any form or by any means, including electronic or photographic reproduction, in whole or in part, without express written permission, except in the case of brief passages embodied in critical reviews and articles.

Illustration art by Doan Trang

ISBN: 978-1-941885-47-5

DEAR READER:

A Sweet Surrender is my debut into historical romance. I'm excited to be re-releasing it with a newly added prologue and epilogue and brand new cover. This short story was written in reverence to America's independence from England, but especially in respect to the "unalienable rights" we are *all* entitled to—life, liberty, and the pursuit of happily-ever-after.

I hope you enjoy this story and the other books in my *Hearts at War* series. Happy reading!

Best,
Lena ♥

For all those who fought and all those who were forgotten.

"Independence is my happiness, and I view things as they are, without regard to place or person; my country is the world, and my religion is to do good."

— THOMAS PAINE

PROLOGUE

Early October, 1777
Upstate New York

The stench of blood and death was strong.

Fear was stronger.

It permeated the cool, autumn air of the ravaged battlefield and hung about as lurid as the groans of the dying men around him.

Not his men, however. None of them were among the dead. They wouldn't be part of his elite cavalry had they made themselves so easy a target.

Sergeant James Blake surveyed the field of dead bodies, not as unaffected by the sight as his demeanor would suggest. But they were in the midst of war and sympathy was a dangerous companion to have in battle. Shrewd ruthlessness and cold indifference was what kept them alive. He needed to remember that and be grateful it wasn't him or his men drawing in their last breath on the cool, damp earth.

Yet, the sight of the nameless enemy combatants that lay slain around him didn't ease the cold pit that had settled in his gut. The familiar uneasiness only expanded until it crawled its way up the nape of his neck.

"Something doesn't feel right about this attack, Sergeant."

James grunted and turned to his corporal. "I agree, Thomas. These men weren't trained to fight."

In fact, the soldiers they had easily defeated had been like sitting ducks, used only as targets to draw the enemy out. Had there been any other way around them, James would have taken it. But they needed to continue north, needed to get to Saratoga if they were to aide General Burgoyne in his campaign to Albany.

A foolhardy mission on Burgoyne's part.

In his hopes to trap the Continental Army in Albany, Burgoyne and his troops were now trapped. Yet, as bold and ill-executed as the general's plan was, James couldn't disobey a direct order. He would lead his men to Saratoga, but he'd be damned if he would walk his men right into an ambush. With his growing apprehension, that was precisely what it felt like.

"Thomas, take the men west and wait for my command," James instructed. "We need to clear that crossing, but I want to be sure there aren't any surprises awaiting us."

It was unlikely that there were, but James

couldn't shake the feeling that they were in a vulnerable position, despite their rivals lying dead around them. No one knew of their progression north—they had only received the missive from General Clinton that morning to make their way to Saratoga.

Thomas frowned. "We cannot afford to have you walk into a trap, Sergeant."

And James couldn't afford to lose any more of his men. His fealty to the crown and his responsibility to his troops kept him fighting in this hopeless war with the colonists. He'd already lost it all. Unlike many of his men, he had no wife, no family, to return home to. The moment he'd held his dying young brother in his arms, he'd given up the folly of ever having that life for himself.

All he had left now was his duty as sergeant to lead his sixty grenadier soldiers to victory in each and every battle.

"Let me ride in your place," Thomas offered.

James shook his head. "With my steed, I will have better luck eluding our enemies if they have indeed plotted such an attack." Only he and several of his men rode astride, including his second-in-command. The others marched afoot. If he was heading into a trap, James could trust the speed and dexterity of his mount to lead him to safety.

"Then let me ride with you."

James shook his head again. "We risk exposure if there are more of us. I will ride ahead and signal you if the path is clear."

"But Sergeant—"

"It is done, Corporal," James said forcefully. "Now wait for my command."

James didn't wait for Thomas' acknowledgment. He veered his horse around and rode north, keeping off the main road. The soft glow of the crescent moon offered little light so he kept his pace slow, fixing his gaze on every shadow as his steed trudged through the dense forest.

The stillness in the air was unsettling, but he welcomed it. Silence didn't mean there weren't savages or colonists lurking about, but they could handle a small group of assailants. It was walking into a well-trained, heavily armed militia that he wanted to avoid.

James stopped and surveyed his surroundings. If they remained on this trail, they could continue their journey through the night and shorten their trip to Saratoga by a day, as was his goal.

As he started back to where his men waited, a whisper of noise darted pass his ear. James spun his head at the sound and it took him a millisecond to recognize the arrow lodged in the tree behind him.

"Bloody hell."

No sooner was the curse past his lips that a sharp pain pierced through his thigh and into his horse's side. The animal screeched and reared up. James tightened his hold on his reins as the horse shot forward into a full gallop. He gritted his teeth at the pain shooting through his leg, but he fought to gain control of the horse. The animal, however, wouldn't be tamed.

Charging through the forest in a mad dash, the large warhorse finally brought them to a clearing. James cursed again as he struggled to calm the wounded animal. He spotted the small army of Bluecoats and veered the horse left.

Right into a trap.

James instantly recognized the familiar crackling of the cannon, but it was too late. The deafening roar splintered through the quiet night as a burst of white light flashed before him. Immense heat followed, scorching his flesh until there was nothing but darkness.

CHAPTER ONE

Two weeks later…

"Siara, don't get too close."

Siaragowaeh ignored the old healer's sharp words and knelt beside the sleeping man. She gently placed her hand on his brow. He was now cool to the touch. She fell back on her haunches in relief. The fever was finally leaving his large body.

"Siara!"

"Don't worry, Etu," she said in their native tongue, preferring their language to that of the English. Though she needed the practice, Etu barely spoke the foreign language and despite the sachem's encouragement to adopt the English tongue in their everyday speech, few of those in their Bear clan did. She turned to the older woman and offered her a reassuring smile. "See, he still sleeps."

"Not for long," Etu grumbled, her thin lips

narrowing further. "My night visions are never wrong. He will rise soon and I see nothing but trouble coming."

Siara hadn't told the old medicine woman about yesterday, when the stranger had woken in a state of confusion and grabbed her arm in a painful grip. It was the first time he had become fully conscious, his eyes wide and wild. Fascinating eyes. As clear and blue as the sky above.

She'd been startled, but not afraid, sensing his fear and need for reassurance. She could only imagine his confusion and delirium. For several days, he had fought the fever while she had tended to the wound on his right thigh. It had taken a gentle touch to his face before he had once again calmed and drifted off into a deep sleep.

The risk she was taking by bringing him here was tremendous. Yet when she had found the wounded, motionless man fighting for his life, she hadn't been able to leave him or turn him over to their clan mother, who would have simply deferred to the chief. Siara had recognized the man's bright red uniform and knew he fought for the other side. Since her tribe now sided with the settlers, they wouldn't care if the wounded man lived or died.

Especially not her betrothed.

Akando had become more ruthless since he'd been appointed the new chief warrior of his clan, the Wolf clan. From what she'd seen of his treatment of captured soldiers, she couldn't possibly trust him with this vulnerable life.

Though Siara had a deep appreciation for all those who breathed, she wasn't ignorant to the ways of the Europeans. They took what they wanted with no regard for those before them. They staked claim on people, land, and things that did not belong to them. They ruthlessly killed and plundered without care or concern. Some of them were not to be trusted.

Yet that did not stop her from helping this man.

She was grateful Etu had agreed to keep her secret about the shrouded campsite they'd constructed around the fallen soldier. The crudely built shelter was supported against a large tree with low hanging branches, keeping it safely hidden. It was wide enough to fit three grown men, giving her and Etu enough room to move. Their secret camp was also a good distance away from their village, and she didn't have to worry about anyone finding them. Not that anyone would venture this far from the village. Many were afraid to wander into these forsaken grounds.

This part of their land had been condemned by the tribe's council members for the many souls that had been lost along its border since the start of the fight between the whites. Yet it was a night vision that had propelled her to come here that fateful day. Her visions were never as consistent as Etu's, and often meant nothing, but she'd come anyway, to pray for the lost souls here. That's when she'd found him, barely clinging to life. Luckily, Etu hadn't been afraid. She had believed they should bury the wounded man, to keep his spirit from living among them, but when he continued to live on through the night, Siara had been filled with hope. She hadn't expected Etu to remain helping her this long, but was extremely grateful for it. With all her gray-haired wisdom, Etu had taught her a lot, but Siara's skill for tending the sick was no match for the experienced healer.

Siara checked the dressing around the man's wound and was pleased to find it still healing nicely. It would scar—there was nothing she could do to prevent that—but it would be no worse than the jagged, puckered mark just below his left rib cage. He had many other faint scars, but none as bad as that one. Though his lean, well-muscled body was riddled with old and new marks, he radiated with life and she was determined to sustain it.

As she reset the dressing on his leg, her gaze unconsciously slid over to the juncture of his thighs and lingered there. While the fever had raged in him, she and Etu had taken turns wiping him down and keeping him cool. Though she had tried to be discreet, she had gotten more than a glimpse of his male member and had been fascinated. He was built like a stallion, long and thick. Even now, it was outlined by the single sheet.

Blushing, Siara glanced away.

She'd seen other men nude during her care of the sick and wounded, but his body was the most magnificent. He was fair, but not as pale as some of the other Europeans she'd come across. The hair on his head and along his jaw was the color of dried grass. Those sprinkled on his chest, arms, and legs were a shade darker. His eyebrows were thick and framed his strong, broad face. A handsome, fascinating face.

Everything about him fascinated her.

"Siara, we cannot keep tending to him much longer," Etu said as she brought over the cup of broth. "More of our men continue to arrive wounded and are more in need of our care. I need to focus my efforts on helping them. Not this one pale face."

"I understand, Etu," Siara said dutifully, taking her place behind his head and gently propping it on her lap. The older woman had been a sort of guardian to her since she'd lost her parents some time ago, and she respected Etu like a grandmother. "I also appreciate your help in this, but I can't give up on him now. Not until he can build his strength to leave us on his own."

How can I abandon him now when he is nearly well?

Grumbling, Etu shook her head, her hunched shoulders stooping further in resignation. Siara paid her no mind as she gently jostled the man awake. He groaned. When his eyes flickered and partly opened, she reached for the cup and tilted it to his lips.

"Drink," Siara whispered softly in English. She slowly and steadily poured the warm liquid into his mouth. "He's getting stronger every day," she said to Etu. That left her conflicted. Though she was delighted to know he was getting better, the thought of him leaving here filled her with a sadness she couldn't place or make sense of. It would be better for her and safer for him if he got well enough to leave their land soon. Yet for the past several days she had nursed him, had nurtured him back to health, and had come to care deeply for him and his well-being—more than she should have.

After he'd taken enough sips to satisfy her, she laid down the cup and ran her fingers over his brows and temples. She enjoyed touching him. With each passing moment, his body hummed with life and strength.

"He will be well soon," she murmured. "I can feel it."

"You will also feel Akando's firm hand on your backside when he finds out about this," Etu retorted.

Siara ignored her and began humming a song meant to comfort and soothe her patient to sleep.

Etu clucked her tongue. "You are threading fire, girl."

Siara glanced up at the old woman with a soft smile. "Everything will be fine, Etu. You will see." She returned her attention to the man and continued running her fingertips along his brows, watching his features soften into sleep.

There was a peace there, where there hadn't been before. He was getting better and that was all she could hope for.

THE BURNING THROB on his leg pulled him from his deep slumber.

Sergeant James Blake steeled himself against the

stabbing pain and slowly took in the sounds around him. He was still alive. A miracle to say the least. The vague sounds of a cannon blast and the faint stench of smoke were still very tangible to him. His body ached and his leg hurt like hell, but he was grateful to be alive.

It was morning now. The loud chirping of the early birds and the smell of fresh dew in the air told him that much. He kept his eyes closed, not moving a muscle. The soft voice that had spoken hours earlier was near. She spoke in a language he didn't understand, but it was her.

His dream woman.

His angel.

No, not an angel. Just a woman. A beautiful woman...but only a woman. He had finally managed to open his eyes yesterday—or had it been the day before? He couldn't remember. Time swirled in his mind, and he lost what little memory he remembered of the ambush that had sent him flying from his horse.

What he did remember was sun-kissed brown skin and large, chestnut-colored eyes.

James continued to lie still when she came near him again. She was alone this time. Whoever it was she had spoken to had left her behind. The woman knelt beside him and briefly placed a warm hand on his cheek. Her light touch on his face and body was soothing—and jarring.

James opened his eyes to slits, peering down at her bent head as she lifted the linen from his naked body. She removed the bandage from his thigh, exposing the wound. He gritted his teeth against the pain of the cool air scraping against his fiery flesh. She applied a slippery salve to the injury, which began to numb the area and chase away the pain. Her movements were deft and unhurried. In the soft morning light, he made out her dark, delicate features. Her long, wavy black hair was braided in two large plaits, though the long strands were pulled to one side of her head, exposing the oak-brown skin of her smooth neck. A slender, elegant neck. One made for kissing.

He wanted to touch her. To pull her over him and nuzzle the tender spot. But he could do neither. His member was willing but his body was beyond weary.

Her slender frame was hidden by her native overdress and skirt, but her perched position left enough of her leg exposed for him to formulate his own thoughts of their softness. He lowered his gaze until he caught sight of the flint knife tied to the sash at her waist. The blade served as a rude reminder that he was defenseless and completely at her mercy.

He didn't like that. In a time of war, that was a dangerous position to be in—something he had learned the hard way and the scar below his ribs was the result of that lesson.

She redressed his wound then replaced the blanket over his exposed body. With fluid grace, she rose to her feet and left. James waited a few minutes before he opened his eyes fully.

A quick inspection revealed that he was in a

crudely built camp with only a blanket beneath him. He gingerly sat up and shifted his leg to test its strength. The salve had helped, reducing the sharp pain to a dull ache. When he attempted to rise, however, he immediately fell back on the blanket. Growling in frustration, he tried again, only to fall back once more, panting. He was still too weak. He would have to wait.

Patience wasn't his strong suit, but he had no choice. He needed to build his strength before he could get the hell out of here.

Had he exercised patience, perhaps he wouldn't have found himself in this uncertain position. He could only hope his sixty grenadier soldiers had not been caught by the surprise blast. He'd ridden ahead of his men as they made their way north to join General Burgoyne's camp, under General Henry Clinton's command. From what he could last recall, Burgoyne's campaign toward Albany was being forestalled and the general had requested immediate assistance in Saratoga to continue on.

However, with the majority of the British regiment still in Philadelphia with General Howe, Burgoyne's plan to take over Albany was ambitious to say the least. James had suggested as much, but under General Henry Clinton's command he had been ordered to ride to Saratoga with his small cavalry of elite assault troops in aid of Burgoyne. But that had been days, perhaps even weeks, since he and his specialized guards had sortied from New York Island, where last he remembered Clinton had been restricted with his own limited reinforcements. They had been close to their destination north, about two days' ride to Albany—or four days to Saratoga if they rode directly.

James needed to know what had happened to his men. His loyalty to them was what kept him fighting in this irrational war. Duty forced him to stay and serve the Crown, but it was his commitment to his troops that demanded he not leave them behind. He'd already failed his brother—he wasn't prepared to fail them too.

Unless the path had been compromised, they would have ridden on. If that had not been possible, Thomas, his second-in-command, would have directed the group to rejoin Clinton. Either way, James would soon need to make his move and continue north.

For now, however, he would wait.

And so he did.

For the next three days, he waited and bided his time until he achieved a stronger command over his body.

The woman continued to tend to him and he learned her schedule. While she was away, he would rise and work on regaining authority over his weak limbs. He was limited in how much he could do, but with each passing moment, he built back the strength in his weak muscles.

When she came near, he would pretend sleep, though it wouldn't be something he would be able to continue much longer. With every touch, every caress, he had to fight with his body to keep from responding.

Her touch was a guilty pleasure he looked forward to each day. And at night…at night, he would lie exhausted on the rough blanket and dream of her.

CHAPTER TWO

It was to Siara's dismay that she learned she was to leave the village in two days' time.

Chief Oskanondonha was arranging a relief party to travel further east to aid the colonists and help tend to the wounded. Each clan was required to provide people and resources and Etu had volunteered her to go.

"Etu, I can't leave him," Siara whispered earnestly, keeping her voice low so others in the longhouse wouldn't hear. "Not yet. You know that."

Etu grabbed her arm and dug her fingers into her. Siara winced.

"You are becoming foolish with this stranger," she rasped in frustration. "Others are beginning to notice you missing throughout the day. Do you know Akando came by the longhouse, and I couldn't account for your whereabouts?"

Siara groaned inwardly. She hated how he exercised his authority over her when they were not wed yet. However, she couldn't ignore the fact that they soon would be. She had managed to ward off his advances as long as she could, but Akando had used his favor with the clan mother and sachem to "encourage" their union. Since she was an untied woman in her prime for child bearing, she had no defenses in denying his request for marriage. But while she was still free of him, she refused to have him rule over her as he tended to do.

"I will deal with Akando," she said to the older woman.

Etu shook her head. "I do not like this. The stranger should have risen by now. If he is trapped in the eternal sleep, there is nothing else you can do for him."

Initially, Siara had the same concern. She had expected the stranger to come fully awake by now, but it had been days since he'd last opened his eyes and seized her in a fevered dream. His color was improving and it took little prompting for him to swallow the broth she fed him and yet he still remained barely conscious. She'd seen men fall to injury and slowly slip into the eternal slumber. Though they still breathed, they never woke again.

But his injury was healing properly and she rarely had to change his bandage. He had even stirred yesterday—or rather parts of him had. She blushed, thinking of it now. The image of his male member thickening beneath the linen cloth was vivid in her mind. She'd been cleaning the area around his wound and his body had responded to her touch in a way it hadn't before, yet when she'd glanced up at his face, he'd showed no signs of awareness.

"Then please promise me you will tend to him while I'm away," Siara said adamantly.

Etu shook her head. "He's not my concern anymore, Siara, and he is no longer yours. In two days' time, you *will* leave with the others."

Siara frowned. Etu had the power to send someone else in her place, but the look in the old woman's dark eyes said she wouldn't concede in this. Though she understood Etu's concern for her attachment to the stranger, Siara didn't understand why the older woman thought sending her away would help matters. She could be gone for weeks. Who would take care of him then?

As she'd done many times now, Siara secretly gathered a few provisions and carefully made her way to the hidden campsite. Etu had stopped coming with her, but Siara continued to go and tend to the stranger on her own. She carried a flint knife with her as she ventured into the condemned woods alone, refusing to stay away as Etu had undoubtedly expected her to.

When she entered the makeshift shelter, it took her a moment to realize the blankets were empty. She froze as panic set in.

Had someone taken him?

A shadow fell over her from behind and she sucked in her breath. Before she could spin around, a hard hand clasped over her mouth, smothering her scream. The small bowl of broth she'd carried slipped from her fingers and crashed to the ground.

"I would hate to have to hurt you, love," a strong, male voice said close to her ear. "But I will if you provoke me."

Siara knew with every fiber in her being that it was the stranger. His nakedness pressed firmly along her backside, though his voice was stronger and clearer than she would have expected it to be. She reached up to peel his hand away from her mouth. She had to let him know that she meant him no harm.

His hand only tightened, jerking her head back against his bare chest. She reached for the flint knife, but he was quick, grabbing it before she could get to it.

"Don't make me hurt you," he said harshly, tightening his arms around her.

Panicked from the hard grip he had around her mouth, Siara swung her arm back. Her fist landed on his bandaged thigh and he drew in a sharp breath.

"Bloody hell."

She pulled away from him and he released her, bracing his weight on his other leg. She struggled internally with her concern for him and fear of potential retaliation. Though she hadn't meant to hurt him, he'd left her no choice.

She made a move for the knife in his hands, but he tossed it away and tackled her to the ground. Everything moved in a blur as she tried to push past him, but he grabbed her by the waist and forced her to the hard earth. He fell over her with a grunt, gripping her wrists and forcing them over her head.

He was stronger than she would have expected. Too strong for someone who had just come from a lengthy recovery.

"Stop fighting me," he growled, his face just inches from hers.

Their breathing came out in harsh pants as they glared at each other. He was sweating and looked a bit wan, and she realized he had over exerted himself. She was suddenly angry that he would undo so much of the progress his body had made these past few days.

"It's you who asks for fight," she snapped, tugging at her arms. "I help you. I *save* you." She added emphasis to her words, trying to make him understand.

He stared down at her, saying nothing, though some of the rigidity had left him. It was then she realized how hard and warm his body was as it pressed her into the ground. Her own body began to soften beneath him, tingling in places it never had before.

He must have experienced the same charge between them because his gaze lowered to her lips. The part of him nestled between her thighs was insistent as it pushed against her.

She tugged at her arms again and he released her, his gaze sliding up from her lips to meet hers. His eyes were the brilliant clear blue she remembered, except there was a heat in them that held her mesmerized. His lips were slightly parted and his face was flushed as he continued to stare down at her...as if he wanted to kiss her.

And she wanted him to.

She held her breath, wanting desperately to feel his lips against hers. But as much as she wanted it, that was something she could not let happen.

Just as he began to lower his head, she placed her hand lightly on his cheek.

"You need rest," she whispered.

With those words, she unraveled the erotic knot that bound them. He rolled away from her and fell onto the disheveled blankets.

She rose to her knees and hovered above him, trying not to stare below his waist as she placed the linen over him. As hard as she tried, it was difficult not to notice his swollen shaft beneath the cloth. She squeezed her thighs together, trying to dull the sudden tingle growing between her legs.

Remember yourself, Siara, she chided herself. Whether she liked it or not, she was to wed Akando. She should not be having such feelings for another.

Before she could inch up the cloth to check on his leg, he grabbed her hand to still her movements.

"Who are you?" he asked, his tone low, but without the sharp bite from earlier.

"I name Siaragowaeh," she said lightly, staring into his piercing blue eyes. "My people just say Siara." Then she repeated his question. "Who are you?"

He hesitated for a moment. "James," he finally said, releasing her hand. "James Blake."

She smiled down at him, finding humor in their polite exchange when only moments ago, they had been grappling around like two irate children.

He lay still as she checked his bandage. Luckily, the wound hadn't opened, but he sucked in his breath at her careful handling.

She looked up at him. "Does it pain?"

"I'll be fine," he said through clenched teeth.

She shook her head, exasperated. He was obviously in some pain. "Mule's head," she muttered, reaching for the jar of healing salve she kept in the tent.

His lips curved slightly, and she found herself drawn to the way the small movement softened his hard features.

"If you mean to call me stubborn," he drawled through his clenched teeth, "I believe the word you're looking for is pigheaded."

Siara nodded. "Yes, you. Pig's head." She focused her attention on his wound, aware of his eyes on her every move. It had been easier to care for him when he had been unconscious, unable to scrutinize her with his penetrating gaze. "I'm sorry I cause you pain," she said quietly. "But you gave me fear."

He jerked slightly as she gently applied the salve. "Then I guess you have nothing to apologize for," he said gruffly.

She glanced up at him again. "How many days you aware?" It was obvious to her now that he had been conscious and quite alert before today.

He was silent for a moment. "A few days now,"

he finally admitted. "Where am I? Where are your people?"

"You are with the Onyota'aka tribe. People of the Standing Stone," she explained. "We good people." Or at least they had been before they had joined sides and decided to ally themselves with the settlers. They were one of two among the six nations to do so, which put them at odds with the other nations in the Iroquois Confederacy. But she didn't explain that all to him.

"How long have I been here?"

She paused, mentally counting the days. "One days plus two weeks."

Once she finished retying his bandage, she was surprised when he began to sit up. She placed her hand on his shoulders, afraid he planned to overexert himself again.

"No, you need rest." She had touched him countless times during her care of him, but touching him while he was fully conscious was a different experience. His broad, muscular shoulders flexed under her fingers, pulsing with strength.

"Sorry, love, but it's not safe for me here."

"No, I make here safe," she argued. "We have distance from village. No one trouble you."

He shook his head slowly. "The longer I stay here, the quicker it will be before someone discovers me." He stared at her for a moment before saying, "I don't know why you've decided to help me, and that puts me forever in your debt. I can only assume, however, if you've hidden me out here, that my presence is not welcomed by your people," he added wryly.

He wasn't strong enough to stand long, much less travel on his own, but he was right, of course. He couldn't stay. Not when she would be forced to join the relief party in two short days and as much as it saddened her, she would have to let him go.

She nodded slowly. "Tomorrow."

He shook his head. "Tonight."

"You need clothes, food, and rest." She pushed down on his shoulders until he fell back on the blanket. "Tomorrow."

He looked as if he wanted to argue, but must have realized the wisdom in her words. "Where are my clothes and pistols?"

With every effort she possessed of his language, she explained to him the condition she had found him in. He had been bloodied and bruised and she had to cut away his singed uniform just to get to his injuries, the most severe of them being the deep laceration on his right leg. His boots had been the only piece of clothing to survive the blast. She had then buried the tattered clothes, along with his weapons, to keep his identity a secret in the event he was discovered.

When she was done with her recount, he stared at her silently, a small frown marring his face. "Why are you doing this?" he asked quietly. "Why are you risking your hide to help me?"

She smiled softly. "Because you needed help. You needed kindness." She rose to her feet, unnerved by his deep, piercing eyes. They bore into her as if trying to read into her soul. She had tried to use the right words to tell him that helping him had been the humane thing to do. No man or animal deserved to die in a ravaged field, bloodied and alone.

"Tonight, I bring more food," she said, avoiding his gaze. "Tomorrow, I find you clothes."

And the day after that, he would return to his people.

It was almost a godsend that she would be among the many preparing for the relief party. No one would suspect her gathering supplies, and she would be able to gather a bit more than usual to give him for his journey back. There was reportedly a British campground west of them, near the Onondaga tribe. Giving him a horse would be too risky, so she would have to break away from the relief party during the expedition, return for him, and take him as close as she dared go.

After, she would rejoin her party.

It was a simple plan. She just needed to wait two more days...

CHAPTER THREE

You needed kindness.

James couldn't shake her words. Kindness was not something he'd had since the start of this damned war. Yet he'd come face to face with it here. With her.

She was wholesome and good, her beautiful dark, slanted eyes filled with nothing but kindness and compassion. Unlike others from this strange land he'd encountered. Most were hardened and jaded—both Natives and colonists alike. However, she appeared to want nothing from him except to aid in his recovery. Such compassion was foreign to him. Nothing in this world came for free. Not even kindness. He needed to remember that.

He also needed a shave.

When the first lights of dawn surfaced, he didn't have long to wait before she arrived with a small meal and clothes for him. Her simple overdress and skirt couldn't thwart his memory of her delicate softness. The memory of her womanly curves cushioning his sexually starved body had left him with a primal need to slide inside her and find mind numbing pleasure.

Outside of his dreams, she was even more spellbinding, more captivating. Her delicate touch and sweet voice sparked a desire in him that had now ignited into a fiery need until he was engulfed by it.

He wolfed down the simple breakfast, then got to his feet and began to dress. His body was growing stronger and the pain in his leg had almost completely faded. She turned away discreetly and he grinned at her unnecessary modesty. While he had been in her care, she had seen him naked countless times. Hell, his manhood had even stirred against her when he'd lain on top of her yesterday. They were beyond modesty now. Except, she was now sexually aware of him. He had recognized the passion in her eyes yesterday. There was a tug of attraction, a definite connection between them, one that she couldn't deny, though she was fighting hard to.

He buttoned up the borrowed trousers then stared down at his exposed ankles and frowned. He was taller than most, broader too. Though those attributes made him an asset as a grenadier solider, it was also a damned inconvenience.

She turned around to face him then quickly hid her mouth with her hand. Her eyes danced with mirth.

"You too tall," she said, shaking her head as she stared at him in his ankle-baring trousers.

He found her amusement contagious and couldn't contain a quick smile. "A blessing and a curse, it appears," he muttered. He didn't bother to put on the shirt. One look at it told him it would be a snug fit. She realized it too and took the shirt from him.

"I find you another."

"I would appreciate it," he said, smiling ruefully. "It wouldn't do for me to walk back to my regime clothed like an ill-dressed savage."

Disappointed anger and resentment clouded her dark eyes and he regretted the thoughtless words as soon as they left him. Though the term was used interchangeably to refer to the Natives, he'd learned over the course of his time in the colonies how degrading the Natives found it.

He cursed and ran his hand over his coarse hair. "I'm sorry, love. I meant no offense." She nodded stiffly, though still visibly upset. "For what it's worth," he added, "I believe all men to be savage brutes."

"Even you?"

The question took him by surprise, but he stared at her directly when he responded. "Especially me."

He had done things, had led men to do things, that no man should be forced to do. Those atrocities would haunt him for the rest of his days.

She slowly shook her head. "I think still some goodness in man."

James couldn't agree. He'd seen men decapitated, gutted, burned, and torn apart—physically and emotionally. He'd watched as his young brother gasped his last breaths, blood pouring from his chest. Death and destruction. All by the hands of men. All in the name of so-called liberty.

But he didn't argue with her. As stupid and dangerous as it was, he found her naive innocence refreshing, even a bit charming.

"Is there a creek you can take me to?"

She thought about it, and then nodded. "But you can relieve yourself behind shrub."

His lips quirked. "I'm quite familiar with the shrub." It was an area he'd visited often enough. "I'd like to freshen up and shave," he explained, rubbing his hand over his jaw. He grabbed a small piece of cloth, the flint knife, and the small container of cream she kept with the healing salve, and then walked up to her. "Lead the way."

They arrived at a narrow, shallow creek down an embankment not too far from the makeshift shelter. He sat down on a rock near the edge of the calm water and for a moment, took in the peace and beauty that surrounded him. After days inside his crude enclosure, he missed the open simplicity of nature.

Siara picked up the cloth he had placed on the ground and dampened it. She came back to where he sat and stood between his legs, her soft breasts inches from brushing against his bare chest. He closed his eyes briefly and breathed in her scent.

Earthy with a hint of sweetness, like flowers and fresh air.

She wiped the cool, wet cloth along his jaw and neck. He stared into her lovely brown face, losing himself in the delicate beauty of her smooth, high cheeks and soft full lips. Her fingers were light as they began to smooth the cream over his overgrown whiskers. His eyes drifted down to her smooth neck where a small, faint pulse throbbed rhythmically. Thoughts of his tongue running along her skin, to the base of her throat made him ache to touch her, to pull her beneath him again until he covered all of her, tasted every inch of her.

When the blunt, sharp end of the blade came into his line of vision, he seized her arm.

"What are you doing," he asked quietly.

"Shave?" she replied, lightly running her free hand through the hairs on his jaw.

Her gentle touch sent a charge so sweet through him that he lost his train of thought for a moment. Tender touch or not, he couldn't let her near his throat with a blade.

"I don't think so, love," he said, carefully extracting the knife from her hand.

She frowned, recognizing the distrust in his action. "I not hurt you," she replied sharply. "I help you."

She held out her hand, waiting for him to return the knife. He continued to stare into her striking, dusky brown eyes. The color of smooth treacle.

Behind those eyes were no devious calculations or masked hatred. Only patient exasperation.

When he didn't move, she sighed and placed her hand once again on his cheek. Her soft touch and gentle eyes lured him, tugging at a place in him he had long thought dead.

"Believe in me," she whispered.

He believed in no one.

But with her, he made an exception. She was sweetness and goodness—and had literally saved his life.

When she reached for the knife, he didn't stop her. He held still as she carefully scraped the blade along his jaw and neck. She trained her eyes on his face, tucking her lower lip between her teeth in concentration. In that moment, he forgot about everything—forgot about the dangers that lurked, his duties to the Crown, and even his men. He simply focused on her. On the alluring lines of her lips, the way her soft hand curved around the side of his neck to hold him still, the way her delicate fingers curved under his chin to shift his head to the side.

Her touch, her nearness, was driving him mad.

Without thinking, he placed a hand on her hip. Startled, she nicked him with a small jerk of her hand. He flinched from the burning cut.

"You must be still," she admonished quietly, wiping the damp cloth over the small cut.

"That's an impossible feat," he murmured, tightening his hands around her. "Especially when I have such a beautiful woman standing so close." He drew her closer until she pressed against him. There was a time he wouldn't have dared taken such liberties with a fine, gentle woman such as her, but that proper British gentleman was long forgotten.

She braced herself against him, her fingers clutching at his shoulder. She stared at him with suppressed passion as he leaned toward her, wanting nothing more than to feel those soft lips against his.

"You mustn't," she breathed, turning away from him.

"Why?" he asked roughly, hating to be denied when they both wanted it bad. "Are you wed?" He didn't believe she was. What husband would let his wife roam the woods without knowing where or with whom she was with? If she were his, he wouldn't let her out of his sight.

"Akando and I will wed once sachem returns to bless union," she said, keeping her gaze lowered.

Jealousy like he'd never known washed over him. He didn't want to think of her belonging to another man, lying with him and letting him touch her.

"Do you love him?"

She glanced up at him in surprise. "It's not matter."

"It matters to me," he said strongly. "I want you, Siara. And I know you want me, too."

Her fingers tightened around his shoulder and her gaze lowered to his lips. Desire pulsated between them, becoming almost tangible. Her breath hitched when he looped his arm around her waist and pulled her to him. Her firm breast pressed against him as he cupped her chin and brought his lips over hers.

The sensation was explosive.

The forgotten blade slipped from her fingers and landed on the ground with a soft thud. She wrapped her arms around his neck and he drowned out everything around them, slanting his mouth over hers, devouring the sweetness of her lips.

He thrust his tongue into her warm mouth and she flicked hers lightly against his, shyly at first then with bolder strokes. He growled low in his throat, his hand cupping the lush curve of her rear and bringing her firmly against him. Straining in the snug trousers, his swollen shaft ground against her, begging for release.

She was a pleasant ache, a devastating distraction…and everything he'd thought she would be. With each tantalizing caress, she grew more daring, straining against him and running her fingers through his hair. Her low, throaty moans drove him wild until the need to be inside her consumed him.

He tugged at the hem of her skirt and she tore her lips away from his, breathing heavily. He slowly moved his lips over her cheek and down her neck, nipping at the tender flesh there. She shivered, her fingers clutching at him. He passed his tongue over the smooth skin, tasting the essence of her, the sweetness of her.

"James…" she gasped into his ear.

The sound of his name coming from her, breathless and filled with passion, made his desire erupt into a need so great, he couldn't stand it. He jerked up her skirt and slid his hand over her bare thighs. She instantly pushed away from him.

"No!" she cried, bringing her hands over her chest and throat. "We mustn't."

Frustration rose in him, but he held himself still, his breath rushing out harsh and fast. He willed his heart to stop its frantic racing. He wanted her back in his arms yet the terrified confusion and anxiety in her eyes kept him from reaching for her. It was a decision he struggled with. Having her in his arms had felt so right.

Carefully, he rose to his feet and walked to the stream. He splashed a handful of water over his face, letting its coolness ease some of the fire raging inside him. Without a word, he went back and collected the knife and discarded supplies.

In strained silence, they returned to the shrouded shelter. As they drew near, the place that had been made to save his life began to feel more like his punishment than his refuge.

Much like the woman walking silently beside him.

CHAPTER FOUR

Her lips still tingled.
Siara had spent much of that morning thinking about James Blake and the passionate kiss they'd shared by the creek. She hadn't known it could be like that—to want a man so fiercely, her body shook with it.

But he was a temptation she couldn't indulge. She belonged to another and would do well to remember that. Tomorrow, James would return to his people and she would travel onto the aid of others.

Siara made her way back to the secluded shelter, carrying the new clothes she had promised James and the supplies for his travel.

As she neared the small camp, angry, muffled shrieks reached her. Panicked, she rushed toward the shelter and came to an abrupt stop at the sight before her. Siara dropped the supplies to the ground and covered her mouth in alarm—then guilty humor.

"James!" she shouted. "Place her down."

Thrown over his shoulder was an angry and violent Etu. The small, old woman pounded on his back with her fist, shouting curses and insults at him, his children, and his future grandchildren.

"Who is this crazy old woman?" he asked, irritated. His arms were wrapped around Etu's legs to keep her from kicking his chest further.

"She is medicine woman," Siara explained. "As me."

"Siara, run!" Etu shouted in their language. "Save yourself from this great beast!"

"Etu, calm yourself. He will not hurt us." She said to James in English, "Please place her down. She has great fear of you."

"It is I who should be afraid," James muttered, easing the old woman to her feet. "The old relic attacked *me* then proceeded to pummel my back blue."

Siara hid a smile as she tried to comfort Etu. She quickly explained to the old woman that he had been awake for some time now—a fact Etu did not appreciate just hearing about—and that she was simply helping him prepare for his return to his people tomorrow.

"Why is she staring at me like that?"

"She doesn't believe to trust you," Siara explained to him. "She has vision that you will do us harm."

James frowned. "Tell her I have no intention of causing anyone harm. You have my word."

"She understands."

As if to confirm, Etu pointed a trembling finger at him. "You. Away. Now."

James raised a brow and Siara moved in front of the older woman. "Etu, please return to the village. I will be there soon."

Etu clucked her tongue and frowned, giving James one more narrowed-eyed look before turning to her. "Remember, you are to travel with the others at first light, Siara. Say your goodbyes to the barbarian and return quickly."

Siara nodded obediently. "Yes, Etu."

Once alone with James, she suddenly became very aware of the two of them in the small space. However, they went on as if that moment by the creek earlier had never happened. She handed him the clothes and he stripped out of the snug trousers. He stood before her gloriously naked. As she'd done earlier, she discreetly turned away. She had managed to find him a longer pair of trousers from the clothes their Colonist allies had supplied them with, complete with a hunting frock.

He dressed himself effortlessly. He favored his better leg while he moved, but he still stood solidly on both. She suspected he would forever have the slight limp and wondered if that bothered him. Once he was fully dressed, he looked similar to one of the neighboring white farmers.

He dug into the simple meal she had prepared. His appetite was big. She hoped she had brought enough to fill him because this was the last meal she would bring him. Tomorrow, he would be gone from here forever.

She pushed her melancholy aside and reveled in her last moments with him. She enjoyed watching him. He looked less like a feral animal with the hair on his face trimmed. She hadn't given him a close shave, not wanting to irritate his skin with the blade, but it would do. The shadow of hair around his face gave him a rugged allure she found dangerously appealing.

He glanced up at her from his bowl when she continued staring at him. "Are there others in your tribe like you?" he asked.

Siara tilted her head to the side, confused. "How you mean?"

"I mean dark," he said plainly, returning his attention to his meal. "I admit I haven't interacted with many Natives, but I expected your people to look more like you."

Siara tensed. He was obviously referring to Etu's olive skin and bone-straight black hair. Whereas, her coloring was of a darker hue and her hair held deep ripples. Though her clan never treated her any different, she had spent most of her life coming to terms with the knowledge that she was a half-breed. In the eyes of others, she was different.

"Don't misunderstand me," he said when she continued her silence. "You're a beautiful woman." He placed his bowl beside him and stared at her thoughtfully. "I guess I'm just trying to understand you," he admitted ruefully.

She studied him, finding only sincere curiosity in his eyes. She guessed then there was no harm in telling him. "My mother Onyota'aka," she began, "and my father African."

He frowned. "Your people allowed this union?"

"My father was brave man," she explained with a tinge of pride. "He danger his life for one of our people, blood son of Clan Mother. As honor, my tribe...how you say, take him inside and make him Onyota'aka."

"Adopt?"

She nodded. "Yes, adopt." Though the tribe always treated her father as one of their own, his dark skin and coiled black hair made him stick out like a pineweed in a dry wheat field. And though her father had embraced the customs of his new family, he had filled her with stories of his home across the ocean, not letting her forget that she had Africa in her blood.

"Where is your father now?"

She looked down at her hands. "He and my mother pass on from sickness." The illness had raged through the tribes, claiming many lives. There were days she missed them fiercely, but there were nights they came to her in her night visions. They often spoke to her, and she took comfort in knowing they were at rest.

"I'm sorry to hear that, love."

Her heart lurched from the tender compassion in his eyes. "Half of me feels deep love and kinship for my people here, for this land. But the other half of me, my father's half, thinks on the land he comes from. I would like very much to know that land," she admitted whimsically.

He gave her a gentle smile. "Perhaps one day we can travel to that part of the world."

She returned his smile. "Yes, perhaps," she said, though they both knew that could never actually come to be. She placed her hand over her heart. "For now, Africa lives here."

He glanced down at her hand, his eyes warm with understanding. Though her physical home would always be here, her heart would always be filled with love for her unknown home. Being far from his own lands, he could obviously relate with her in that, and she loved him for indulging in her fanciful thoughts.

She froze.

I love him.

Her heart fluttered for a moment. It was freeing to finally admit those feelings to herself, even if a love between them could never exist. In the weeks she'd cared for him, there had been a strong connection between them. One that had compelled her to venture into these forsaken grounds and find him. Now that bond trembled from the tension of its inevitable break.

Siara didn't want to leave him, but it was getting late and she had stayed away far too long. His wound was completely healed now and didn't require her attention any longer. If anything, he was now capable of tending to it himself, which he had been. He didn't need her anymore.

Heavy hearted, Siara rose to her feet. He followed suit.

"We leave tomorrow at first light," she said quietly.

He gave her a curt nod. "I need my pistols, love."

"Yes. Tomorrow."

"No. Tonight."

She sighed in frustration. She hadn't forgotten, but she hadn't had the time to unearth his weapons and carry them back to him. With darkness also coming soon, there was no way she could get them now. When she explained that to him, he finally relented.

"I am once again completely at your mercy," he muttered. "Go then. I'll wait for you tomorrow at dawn."

She nodded and gathered her items. She started toward the opening, but he reached out and took her hand in his.

"Siara."

She turned to him, a warm feeling passing through her at the sound of her name coming so affectionately from his low, deep voice.

"Thank you," he said simply.

Something softened inside her and she gave his hand a gentle squeeze. "You are much welcome." Instead of releasing her, he pulled her closer. She read the longing in his eyes and wanted nothing more than to be with him. Moving without thought, she took another step toward him.

Suddenly they both froze at the sound of a horse approaching.

"Siara!"

Her heart sank as she recognized the voice. Akando. She glanced behind her, toward the opening of the shelter, then back at James.

"Stay here," she whispered fiercely before rushing out to meet Akando.

"Siara?" Akando rode up to her, his glare sharp and unwavering. "I've been searching everywhere for you. Why are you out here alone? You should be preparing with the others for the journey tomorrow."

"I am already prepared," she replied coolly, hoping he couldn't see her nervousness. "I just wanted some time alone."

He frowned, glancing around them. "Here? This is not a safe place for you. Come. Let's—" He glanced behind her and gestured toward the shelter. "What is in there?"

"Nothing," she said, walking toward him. "Just a place for me to rest." She managed to control the anxious quiver in her voice, but there was a suspicious glint in his gaze as he stared hard at the crude shelter.

"I see something in there…" He slid down from his horse and her anxiety increased tenfold as he headed toward the shelter. When he walked past her, she grabbed for his arm.

"Akando, it's nothing," she said earnestly.

"Please. I would like to return to the longhouse now."

But he ignored her, shaking her hand away. She stood there frozen, unsure what to do. If she called out a warning, what then? She didn't want either man hurt.

After a brief, internal struggle, she followed him. Maybe if she explained, tried to convince him the rightness in what she'd done, he wouldn't harm the injured man lurking inside.

But James wasn't lurking.

He rushed out, wrapping Akando with the blanket that had been kept inside. Akando let out a shout and fell back. James pulled out the flint knife, looking ready to charge toward the fallen man.

Akando quickly swept the blanket from his body and bounded to his feet. He was as tall as James and lean with muscle. She caught a glimpse of the tomahawk in his hand and the bottom of her stomach dropped. She ran toward them, her arms stretched out between the two men to keep them from advancing toward each other.

"Please stop this," she shouted at James in English.

"Damn it, Siara," James said fiercely. "Step away."

She shook her head. "James, I will explain for him why. There will be no need for fight." She turned to Akando and switched to their language. Though Akando's English was superior to hers, it would be easier and quicker for her to explain. "Please don't hurt him. He was wounded and I cared for him. That is all. He is not strong enough to do you any harm."

Akando didn't take his eyes off of James when he asked sharply in English, "You brought this white man here?"

She swallowed then nodded, well aware that admitting to such a crime would result in a severe punishment. Possibly even exile.

"Yes, but only because he was terribly hurt."

"He appears quite fit to me," Akando snapped.

"He has only just gotten better," she said frantically. "He is preparing to leave here and return to his people."

"Only to bring them back here to raid our village," he spat, advancing toward James, his grip tight on the tomahawk.

Siara pushed against his chest with all her might. "No!"

Akando jerked away from her, his face twisted with rage. "Treacherous whore!"

She wasn't prepared for the blow that came next. His fist connected with her jaw with such force, she tasted blood. She lay sprawled on the ground, dazed and her ear ringing. She vaguely realized she had bit her tongue.

A low snarl rumbled above her and in a blur, the two men landed with a loud thud on the ground beside her. James straddled Akando and landed blow after blow onto his face and chest.

Siara scrambled to her feet and rushed to the struggling men. As James prepared to bring his fist down again, Siara rushed behind him and grabbed his raised arm.

"James!" she shouted, her voice cracking. "Please, no!"

He stopped and looked up at her. His eyes burned with a steely rage that took her breath.

Akando used that brief moment of distraction to slam his fist into James chest. Surprised by the sudden attack, James flew back against her with a loud grunt. She had no time to move away. Struggling to maintain her footing, she tripped over a raised tree root and went flying to the ground.

Akando released an ear-piercing battle cry and the last thing she witnessed, before her head struck something smooth and hard, was James trapped beneath the warrior and his raised tomahawk.

JAMES WATCHED as the spiked-end of the tomahawk started down between his eyes. He kicked out at the warrior's hand, knocking the vicious looking ax from the man's grip. A second longer and it would have found a home in his skull.

James swung his other leg behind the man, forcing him back to the ground. He came over the man again and began landing blow after blow, beating him mindlessly, determined to finish him.

He'd struck Siara. He deserved to die.

But the warrior was strong. He managed to roll away from under James and crawl toward the tomahawk. James reached for him, but was too late.

Akando clutched the tomahawk in his fists. James fell over him and wrapped his arm around the man's neck, keeping him on his stomach. The man gurgled and strained beneath him as James increased the pressure and held him in the fierce grip. With his free hand, he wrenched the tomahawk from Akando's hands. For a moment, James debated whether he should slam the blade into the man's skull or simply snap his neck and be done with it.

I have no intention of causing anyone harm.

His words echoed in his head, jarring him out of his murderous rage. He'd made that promise to Siara—a promise he was seconds away from breaking. And she would hate him forever.

Suddenly, he remembered her sharp cry and fear flooded him.

Siara!

He turned to find her lying on the ground, unmoving. He released the unconscious warrior and pushed away from him. A moment longer and he could have strangled the warrior to death. He wasn't all that convinced that he shouldn't.

Instead, James rushed to Siara's side. She was still breathing and he experienced a relief so great, he shuddered with it.

"Wake up for me, love," he prompted hoarsely, brushing the loose strands of hair from her face. "Come on."

She moaned softly, wincing as her eyes fluttered open. He scanned her body, to see if there were any obvious injuries. "Tell me where it hurts, love."

Siara lifted her hand to her head. James ran his fingers gently through her hair until he brushed against the knot beginning to form. She winced again and moaned. He withdrew his hand.

"My head," she croaked. "It's hurt."

"I know, love. Can you stand?" They couldn't linger there much longer. The warrior was bound to wake up soon—if his battle cry hadn't already alerted others.

When she struggled to her feet, James swooped her into his arms, bracing his weight on his good leg. He would not leave her here. Not to face retribution at the hands of her people just because she had saved his life. He carried her to the warrior's horse and placed her atop it. "Wait for me," he said. He grabbed the flint knife and the tomahawk and headed into the crude shelter that had been his dwelling for the past few weeks. He quickly gathered the supplies Siara had prepared for him and headed back to her. The warrior began to stir just as James climbed up on the horse behind her.

Without another look back, he veered west and rode off through the heavy forest. The warrior's faint shout faded behind them, but James continued his neck breaking speed, holding Siara tight. He rode for a good distance before it was safe enough for them to slow. Siara's arms remained wrapped around him and he looked down at her. Her eyes were closed. He would have thought she'd fallen asleep if she hadn't been holding on to him as if she were afraid to let go.

He would soon need to find a place for them to

take shelter for the night, but apprehension prevented him from stopping. The warrior may very well be on their trail. James planned to circle their tracks to throw off any scouts who may possibly follow them. He didn't like to be without his pistols and would have to hope they didn't run into any hostile Natives or militiamen.

James wasn't familiar with the land and couldn't be certain they were on friendly native grounds. If he took her with him to a British encampment, they would have to venture into other native lands to do so, some who may be welcoming, some who could be downright hostile.

He hadn't planned to have her with him during his journey back, and taking her only increased the possibility that her tribe would come after him to get her back. His arms reflexively tightened around her.

She was his now.

It had been tough thinking about never seeing her again or having to leave her behind. If that bastard who'd struck her was her betrothed, James thought with disgust, then he didn't deserve her.

But having her with him meant James would have to change his plans. If he remembered correctly, Albany was only a two day ride from where they were. There, it was about another two to Saratoga. He didn't dare continue to Saratoga. Instead, he would take them to Albany and send out a missive. He'd lost over two weeks during his recovery and didn't want to risk walking into enemy territory. With his Yankee clothing, it wouldn't be difficult for him to mask himself as a simple farmer if they happened to run into trouble.

With one horse, it would take them maybe another day to get to Albany. By then they would surely run out of food and supplies. If that happened, he would have to scavenge to get what they needed. The horse would soon need to rest, as would they.

"How's your head, love?" he asked quietly.

She opened her eyes and stared up at him. "Better some." But her brows were pulled together in agitation and worry. "James, you must take me back."

He looked down at her. In his contentment of having her with him, he hadn't factored in that she may not want to leave. He lightly touched the swollen bruise on the side of her face and frowned. "Why? He will only hurt you again."

She glanced away. "But... I just cannot leave my people."

He gave her a gentle squeeze, understanding what she was feeling. Loyalty and duty tended to come with their own heavy shackles.

"We can't go back, love. I've already escaped death twice. I'm not prepared to test fate a third time."

CHAPTER FIVE

They rode in silence for what seemed like forever.

Siara was being torn apart by her guilt and regret. Regret for the trouble she had caused and the worry her absence would surely bring Etu. Guilt for leaving her home and people, yet wanting nothing more than to be with James.

She leaned against him, seeking out his heat. The winds had picked up and there was a distinct chill in the air. Tightening her arms around him, she buried her face in his chest and breathed in his scent. He leaned down and kissed her gently on the top of her head. It was a subconscious action, one she didn't think he realized he'd done, but it made her smile through her gloom.

Her headache was now reduced to a dull throb, though her cheek still stung. But it was the mounting pain from sitting on the horse in such a position that was truly starting to bother her.

By the time they stopped, the sun had completely fallen from the sky and they were shrouded in darkness. James found a small clearing deep in the forest for them to camp for the night. Because he didn't want to risk drawing unwanted attention, they prepared their small camp under the guidance of the moonlight.

She hesitated when she realized they would have to share the single blanket.

"Come, love," he said, his hands held out to her. "We're both exhausted."

She slid her hand into his and he pulled her down on the blanket where he held her close. Held her as if he had no intentions of letting her go.

Yet she woke the next morning to find that he had.

She rose from the blanket and found him readying the horse. She freshened up at a small pond nearby then gathered their supplies and came up to him.

"Here," he said, handing her some of their provisions. "Eat."

She reached for the berries and corn bread. "Now it's you who care for me," she teased him at their now reversed roles.

He didn't return her humor. "Yes, I do," he said quietly staring at her in a way that made her heart quiver and her face flush.

Shortly after they finished their simple breakfast, they climbed on the horse and started their journey through the dense forest. There was a distinct chill in the air, however, that said a storm was coming. The sun had yet to peek through the clouds, and though she suspected rain had begun to fill them, the many trees above them prevented her from knowing for sure.

"Where do we go?" she eventually asked, breaking the silence that had seemed to follow them since they'd left her village. Though she understood the need for him to remain vigilant of their surroundings as they traveled the rough terrain, there was a new stoic alertness about him that she wasn't accustomed to.

"We're going north," he explained. "To Albany. There, I'm hoping to get news of the current state of the conflict and find out what happened to my men."

"Then what after?"

He looked down at her, silent for a moment. "I don't know. What would you want?"

She stared at him, puzzled. She didn't know either. All she knew for certain was that she loved him and wanted to be with him.

But that could never be. Not when they lived in two separate worlds.

Before she could respond, a fat raindrop landed on her face. Suddenly the clouds broke open and released a deluge of water. James tried to shield her from the pounding rain with his large body, but it was no use. By the time they found refuge in a shallow cavern at the base of a bluff, they were both drenched.

"Wait here," James shouted over the thunderous rain. He went back to find a place to tether the horse.

Laying their blanket and supplies down, Siara stood at the wide opening of the rock shelter. Her wet, wavy hair hung down around her like a dark curtain and she watched as sheets of rain pounded the earth. She shivered from the cold wind whipping through her wet clothes and stepped further back into the cavern.

She kicked off her wet moccasins, undid her wrap skirt, and wrung out the excess water. She found a dry spot to spread out the damp material then grabbed the hem of her tunic and wrung out as much of the water as she could. The wet overdress still clung to her hips and breasts despite her efforts. But she didn't dare remove it and risk James finding her stark naked.

A shadow fell over their small rock shelter and Siara spun around to find a soaked James standing at the mouth of the entrance. He shook himself like a feral animal and began to pull off his clothes. When his hands went to his trousers, Siara turned away.

Did he mean to get fully naked now!

It was ridiculous of her to feel appalled by the idea. She had already seen him naked more than a few times, but things had been different between them then. He'd been either too sick to do anything or had immediately changed into clothes. But now... how was she to ignore him when her body throbbed just from the sight of him?

She tried, nonetheless. Oh, did she try.

Fully naked, he looked out at the still raging storm. At the first glimpse of his strong, muscular back, she couldn't look away. Her eyes slowly moved down his broad back and down to his firm, muscular backside. The gray glow of the overcast skies created an impressive silhouette of his imposing, virile form.

He truly was magnificent.

"We'll wait here until the storm passes before we start again," he said over his shoulder.

She didn't respond to him. She couldn't. Her voice was trapped in the back of her throat, and her legs trembled from the tightly clenched muscles of her thighs. She wanted to touch him, but didn't dare. It would only make it that much harder when they eventually parted.

Akando had cursed her "whore" and maybe he was right. Her body lusted for a man that wasn't her husband, yet no amount of self-rebuke—or thigh clenching—could ease her ache.

When he turned to her, naked desire pulsed through her. Plain for him to see.

They stood facing each other in silent yearning. She stared down at his member, which jutted from his body, broad and rigid. Her breath caught and her lips parted slightly as the pulsing between her thighs grew stronger.

She took a deep, shuddering breath and the small

action broke what restraint he had left. With a growl, he stalked toward her. She backed away, trying to fight the yearning that threatened to dismantle the little resolve she struggled to hold on to.

"James, no," she whispered breathlessly. "I am to belong to Akando."

But he ignored her, continuing his advance until her back came up against the stone wall. He cupped her chin and brought her gaze to his. Her nipples hardened at his touch, his nearness.

"You belong to me," he said gruffly. "You are mine, Siara."

She stared into his striking blue eyes and something inside her crumbled. Denial was futile, yet she attempted it anyway.

"No," she murmured weakly.

His eyes flashed. "Yes," he rasped then hauled her up to his hard chest. His lips came down on hers, hot and heavy, and she surrendered to the desires of her body. To him.

They pulled away only long enough for him to remove her tunic. For a brief moment, he stared down at her before he reached out and cupped one of her breasts. She sucked in a gasp of intense pleasure, her nipple stabbing against his palm.

"So beautiful," he murmured as he molded his hand around the plump flesh. He rubbed his thumb over the sensitive bud then brought his lips over to her other breast and pulled the straining nipple into his warm mouth.

Pleasure like she had never known coursed

through her. A deep moan wrenched from her as her head fell back against the stone wall, eyes closed. She brought a hand up to his head and ran her fingers through his thick hair. Her other hand clenched around his broad shoulders, holding him as her legs trembled fiercely beneath her.

He continued his tortuous tease, flicking his tongue over the small, sensitive flesh then sucking strongly.

"James," she gasped. "Please." She didn't know what she was pleading for, but only that he could quiet the storm of desire raging inside her.

His arms tightened around her waist as he trailed his lips up her breast and to the base of her neck. He lingered there for a moment before he brought his lips back over hers. She kissed him as if it was their first time, taking in the heady taste of him. His shaft strained against her belly, hot and heavy and pulsing with life. She reached down and wrapped her fingers around his rigid shaft. He shuddered violently.

The power she held in her palm was exhilarating. She squeezed and caressed his hard length until he suddenly jerked away.

"I need to be inside you, love," he said thickly.

"Yes," she agreed softly. She needed him, too. She needed his possession as much as she needed her next breath.

He lifted her in his arms and her legs instantly wrapped around his narrow hips. He carried her to the ground, onto her outstretched skirt, and knelt between her thighs. A moan wrenched deep from her throat when he slipped a blunt finger into her tight, wet core. He slid it out of her slowly then thrust into her again.

She gasped, her body tightening around his stroking finger, her rising hips seeking out more of the delightfully intense sensation. Her moans echoed around them in the dim cavern as he brought her to fevered heights.

With a harsh groan, he widened her legs and moved over her. Bracing himself on one arm, he reached down between their bodies with the other and began guiding himself into her, pushing through her tight channel. His breathing was harsh and labored as he continued his slow thrust, stretching her. She cried out as a moment of intense pain sliced through her, piercing her haze of pleasure.

Leaning down, James kissed her again, reigniting the gut-wrenching desire that tugged within her. Her body trembled and tightened around him and he groaned deeply. With his soft kisses, caresses, and whispered words of affection, her body eventually softened around him and adjusted to his deep penetration.

He began pushing into her, slowly at first, but as the intense pleasure engulfed them, he lifted her hips and began driving into her. Their bodies melded together as he continued his heavy thrusts, his harsh groans mingling with her soft gasps. With every stroke, he brought her to new, unimaginable heights, his deep thrusts building a tension in her belly that grew unbearably tight. He grunted as she clawed his muscular back and bit his shoulder, needing to find some relief from the intense desire surging inside of her. With one strong, deep thrust, she arched her back and came apart with a muted scream, her body trembling uncontrollably. He fell over her and let out a low, harsh groan as the heat of his release filled her.

Panting, they lay on the stone ground unmoving, still joined together—by body and heart. The storm had passed—both inside and outside the cavern—and the rhythmic sound of the lingering rain filled the now still air. She stroked his back as he burrowed his face in the crook of her neck, pressing his lips softly against the base of her throat.

Holding him close, Siara finally understood that she did belong to him.

And he now belonged to her.

JAMES GATHERED Siara close as they lay cocooned in the single blanket. The storm had eased to a quiet drizzle, but there was a chilly bite in the air. He attempted to let the heat from his bare body chase away the cold because he did not dare build a fire. Not with imminent threats surely lurking near.

Siara nestled closer to him and released a soft breath. He shut his eyes, absorbing the delicate sigh. Her gentle breathing indicated she still slept deeply and he dared not wake her. Because of the storm, they had lost a day of travel, but he couldn't regret this small reprieve. Not when she needed it so.

The past few days of travel had been rough and he had done more than just push her beyond her limits—he had irrevocably changed the course of her life. It was just as well since she had forever changed his.

James knew it wasn't guilt he felt over taking her away from her home—he didn't think he could ever regret having her with him—but he did feel a sense of responsibility toward her. It was now his duty to protect and provide for her.

Initially, he'd had misgivings as to whether he was capable of that. He was a man with a lame gait, a stolen horse, and a plan that hinged on safely crossing through enemy territory. Beyond that, he'd had no clear future for himself or the woman he had just claimed.

But the storm had changed that.

It had forced them into this small shelter where he had been able to stop and think—and acknowledge a simple yet fundamental truth.

He was no longer alone.

In just a few hours, he had gained that single clarity and it had changed everything. He no longer wanted to be the kind of man that followed blindly, as if he had nothing left to lose. He now had Siara, and the possibility of a future with her made his heart thump heavily in his chest.

James had long ago abandoned fanciful thoughts of ever having a family that the prospect of such a life felt foreign to him. Yet, now he had never wanted anything so desperately.

Peering down at Siara, he realized that he now had someone to live for and a lot to lose. The thought filled him with such yearning that it terrified and exhilarated him. He could only hope that she wanted the same thing.

CHAPTER SIX

The travel to Albany was taking longer than they anticipated.

After the storm had passed, they'd traveled for three days and had yet to arrive. According to James, they still had another day or so. He claimed the frequent breaks they took were to rest the horse, but from the way he watched her, Siara believed some of his concern was for her as well. They had also gone from traveling during the day to now making the journey at night, under the pale glow of the moon. It was to avoid potential detection, he'd said, but it only added to their slow pace. She hadn't expected the journey to be easy, but after last night, she was anxious to get to their destination.

She tried to forget the carnage they had come upon. It appeared to have been the aftermath of a terrible raid on a camp that had resulted in bodies everywhere. Those who had not yet passed on had been crying out in pain, some praying, begging for mercy. She hadn't been able to tell who side those men had been fighting for—and it hadn't mattered. She wanted to go to them, to help those she could. But James wouldn't allow it. He reminded her that she wasn't equipped to help any of them and that it wasn't sensible or safe for her to even try.

Though he had been right, it hadn't lessened her pain. He had held her as she sobbed for the lost lives and broken spirits. With two more days' ride stretched before them, James had decided to scavenge for more supplies and weapons. They had passed a small town not too far from where she now hid. She wanted to go with him, but he'd argued he'd have a stronger chance of success if he didn't have her to worry about. He'd found a secluded area to hide her and the horse, leaving her with the flint knife and instructions to stab anything that came near, then "ride like hell" toward the North Star. If he managed to find another horse, he wouldn't be far behind.

But she hated the wait.

This was the first time they'd been apart since the start of their journey. She had grown accustomed to having him near. Being alone now left her feeling strange and uneasy.

She sat with her back pressed against a large tree, clutching the sharp weapon in her hand and watchful for signs of his return—or unwanted company. The departure from her village felt like it had happened long ago instead of only a few days.

She had longed to speak to Etu, to ease the woman's worry, and on the second night after their departure, Siara had gotten that chance. She closed her eyes and smiled, remembering the night Etu had come to her in a night vision. They had spoken and Siara had assured the older woman that she was safe—but she was following her heart.

In the short time she and James had spent together, they had grown close—closer than she'd ever been with anyone. The bonds of the flesh had a way of doing that. Yet it was the aftermath that solidified their unity. She learned more about him as he opened his heart to her and shared his past, including the time he'd befriended a traitor who had left him with that horrible scar on his rib. She also learned that he'd had a younger brother, Matthew, who'd died fighting in this war. The remorse of having to watch his only close relative die and the guilt for not being able to protect him was still very fresh. Her heart broke for him, but she let him know, without words, that he was no longer alone.

After tonight, she never wanted them to be apart this long again.

She didn't know how long she waited before her eyes began to grow heavy. A faint rustling in the dense trees forced her to alertness. Her eyes widened as she kept them trained in the direction of the noise. It could have been just a scared animal scurrying away.

Scurrying from what, though?

James hadn't left from that direction, so she didn't

expect him to be returning that way. When the noise came again, Siara jumped to her feet, her heart pounding in her chest. She kept the flint knife firmly in her grip as she waited for the impending attack.

What came next shocked her and she nearly dropped the knife. One by one, men wearing what resembled the uniform of the British Army appeared before her, until they surrounded her small hiding space. There were as many as fifteen or twenty of them. Their usual bright red coats and white trousers were dark with blood and filth. They were all large, fierce-looking men and her heart raced faster.

When one of the men advanced toward her, she raised the knife in front of her. There was no way she could get to the horse with so many of them near. There was also no way she could fend them all off, but she would die before she let any of them touch her.

"Wallace, bring the light," the man standing before her said. His hair was as dark as night, but his eyes had a pale glow.

"I believe it's a savage woman, corporal," another behind him said.

Anger sprang up in her at the insult. She was no savage. She was Siaragowaeh. Onyota'aka and Africa ran through her blood. Before she could correct his ignorance, a small lantern flared to life. The man they called "corporal" raised the lantern to her face. She flinched from the sudden bright glow.

"Do you speak English, woman? Are you alone? Where is your man?"

Siara debated whether she should respond. Would it be in her best interest if they didn't know she could speak their language?

Before she could make a decision, the man must have lost his patience because he handed the lantern to another and started toward her again. She had no desire to do anyone harm, but she would do what she must to protect herself. His steps were determined and Siara backed away from him, the knife raised to attack. That didn't deter him.

"*Thomas.*" James' harsh shout sliced through the quiet, tense air just as the man reached for her. "Don't you dare touch her."

JAMES DROPPED the sack he'd carried and made his way toward Siara. When he'd seen the glow of the lantern flare to life in the distance, he'd been struck with such mindless fear, it had left him frozen. But only for a second. He'd never run so fast in his life and was grateful he hadn't fallen and broken his neck trying to get to her.

"Back away from her," he snapped, coming to stand in front of his second-in-command. "*Now.*"

The corporal backed away, his face a mask of stunned disbelief. It was obvious his men were just as shocked to see him as he was to see them. There would be time for questions and explanations later, however.

He turned to Siara and cupped her chin. He hated

the fear his men had put there. "Are you all right, love?" he asked, staring down at her searchingly.

She nodded, her eyes glistening. He pulled her in a quick hug before he turned to face his men. Or what was remaining of them. The number that stood there now was only a quarter of what he remembered.

"Sergeant Blake? How are you alive?"

He laced his fingers through Siara's hand and glanced at each of his men before he spoke. "I'm alive because of this woman here. Her name is Siara. She is under my protection and all of you will give her the respect and civility you would any gentlewoman."

Every one of them nodded, though a few looked at him still in wonder and amazement.

"We found your horse," Thomas said, among those still dazed. "Or what was left of it. We believed surely you had been blown apart by the blast too."

"Well, as you can see, I'm still very much whole," James said wryly. Except his leg. Despite his recovery, he was left with a slight limp and on occasion, it would ache mildly. His mad dash through the forest had now brought on a dull throb. "But I lost two weeks of consciousness, so you will need to fill me in on what happened."

"A group of militiamen had been responsible for the blast," Thomas explained. "When it went off, we rushed to your aid. But when there was no sign of your body, we began our retreat."

"Back to New York Island?" James asked.

Thomas nodded. "We couldn't be sure the rest of

the path to Saratoga hadn't been compromised and I wanted us to get back to General Clinton so that he could be informed of our setback and your…demise."

More like his failure, James thought with some regret. It had been his responsibility to lead his men, and he had led them straight into an ambush.

"Why are you not there, then?"

"We were captured," the corporal said with disgusted frustration. "Held on the outskirts of Saratoga. But when word arrived several days ago that Clinton had come up the Hudson River and claimed two forts there, the Continental Army made their way to Albany to halt his advancement. That gave us the opportunity to make our escape."

"What happened to the rest?" James asked, glancing around the small group.

"Some were killed during our combat with the rebels." He looked uncomfortable when he finally confessed, "And some decided to renounce their duties to the Crown and migrate west."

James should have been surprised by that, but he wasn't. His men were loyal to the Crown and would give their life for their country, but he understood more than many how heavy the cost of loyalty could be. He had lost everything he'd known because of this war. His only family, his home. Himself.

But in Siara, he was rediscovering the essence of who he was—and he found something truly worth fighting for. In the days he'd known her, he'd come to realize that he loved her fiercely for the affection and renewed life she'd given him. He couldn't stand to lose her, too.

"Clinton must have discovered our captivity hence his sudden decision to make a move toward Albany," Thomas continued. "But it was a daring effort made in vain."

James frowned. "What do you mean?"

Thomas' sigh was heavy. "Word arrived the night before we escaped that Gentleman Johnny has surrendered Saratoga," he said ruefully.

James' eyes widened in surprise. This was surely the first. His Majesty's army had never surrendered a battle before.

"I cannot say I blame the general," Thomas continued. "The Continental Army had risen to almost three times that by the time he'd laid down his arms. Whether we'd made it there in time or not, there was little chance we would have won that battle."

James nodded, taking some solace in his words. He glanced around at what remained of his group. Though he regretted the lives lost, he was glad to see many of them had survived to live and fight another day.

"What will you do next, Sergeant?" Thomas asked. "Will you return with us to New York Island?"

James looked down at Siara and gave her hand a gentle squeeze. They may have lost this battle, but he'd won so much more. His life, as he knew it, was forever changed.

"I believe that is something I will have to discuss

with my wife," he said, smiling down at Siara's astonished expression.

Thomas eyes also widened in surprise, but then he graciously offered his congratulations. "Well then, I wish you two good health and Godspeed."

Having been trained well by him, his men had also been traveling at night and had come upon the secluded spot for a moment's rest. James made arrangements with his men to camp close with them tonight. The added protection wouldn't hurt and in the morning, they would all go their separate ways.

It was fate and perseverance that had brought his men to him. Now, he could move on from them and focus on his future with the woman at his side.

Once alone and nestled in the roll of their blanket, James held Siara close. He wasn't surprised when her question came.

"James, why do you lie and call me your wife to your friends?"

He tightened his arms around her and placed a kiss on her forehead. "Because in the eyes of God, you are my wife."

Every time she opened for him, every time he came inside her and shared in the limitless pleasure of becoming one with her, she became more his.

"Will you take me to your lands, then?" she asked quietly. "Show me your home?"

He placed his hand under chin and peered down at her through the moonlight. "Is that what you want?" he asked. "I know you love this land. Are you prepared to leave it forever?"

She shook her head. "I love *you*, James. It is you I can't bear to leave."

His heart filled with warmth for her. She didn't know what those words did to him. He leaned down and kissed her softly. "I love you too, sweetheart." He kissed her again, then leaned back down and stared up at the bright stars peppering the dark sky. "So where should we go, Siara? Do you want to sail the seas to England or stay in this land? Do you want to continue north, perhaps? Go to Canada? Or take our chances out west?"

She was silent for a moment. "There are so many to choose," she said quietly.

"I know," he agreed. Above them, a crescent moon glowed against the black sky. He took her hand and brought it up to his lips. "I would get you the moon if that's what you wanted, love. Just tell me your heart's desire, and I will try my damnedest to fulfill it."

It was at that moment that he truly understood the desire for liberty, for the freedom to pursue a semblance of happiness, because he would gladly migrate to the ends of the earth with her.

She took their locked hands and placed it over her heart. "What of Africa?"

He looked down at her, prepared to tell her he'd never made the voyage, but they could do so together. Whatever she wanted. But from the loving, teasing glint in her eye, he finally understood and smiled.

For her, Africa was where her heart was. A home

she'd never known. A trip she'd always wanted to take. He had offered that to her—a journey to a place unknown. So long as they made the voyage together. It didn't really matter where they decided to go next because home was where *they* were.

"Africa it is, then," he murmured, hugging her close.

EPILOGUE

Late December, 1781
Four years later…

"It is our duty and destiny to protect the colonies from rebel scum!"

James spared the man a glance before returning his attention to his drink. The tavern was filled with tired men looking for warmth and respite from the bitter cold outside. Instead, they had to suffer through the ramblings of a drunk dressed in a ranger's uniform. James could only hope that the intoxicated man would take himself and his near empty bottle of gin elsewhere.

"We will fight to the death," the ranger continued, his slurred voice raising an octave. "We will fight until we have reclaimed our lands for our families and for our country. God save the king!"

James ignored the sporadic shouts of support that

resounded around the tavern. The man was arguing for what was a lost cause by many accounts. Despite recruitment efforts from brutal militia units like Butler's Rangers, the Royal defense was said to have weakened and was swiftly losing its hold over the colonies.

Reports of Britain's defeat in Yorktown had managed to reach their isolated corner of eastern Canada, yet that had not deterred some, like this drunkard, from voicing their continued fealty. In his estimation, the British army's ultimate surrender in Virginia was a devastating blow to the Crown. They would need more than just a group of ill-trained, unregulated men to win this relentless war. They would need a miracle.

"What say you, Blakemore?"

James glanced up at his neighbor Benjamin Marshall, a large, barrel-chest of a man, as he fell into the available seat at his table.

"Will you join your king's men in battle for one last victory?"

"Will you?" James countered.

Ben scoffed. He was a former slave who had enlisted to fight for his freedom under Lord Dunmore's Proclamation, but had done like many in their quiet settlement and taken his destiny into his own hands.

"This is not my fight. Your king promises freedom for those slaves who fight against the very men who seek their own liberty. Yet, it is not independence for all men that the colonists fight for. Such hypocrisy is offensive. As I see it, I'm better off trusting neither side."

James nodded. "Our sentiments on this matter then are shared. This is no more my fight than it is yours."

Many of their neighbors and the men James worked alongside in the fields held similar attitudes. Their settlement was largely made up of deserters, runaway slaves, and displaced Natives who were primarily motivated in rebuilding their lives and securing their own liberty and happiness. As their mixed-race community grew, it was becoming apparent that many wanted no part in the conflict. It was only a matter of time before a final, blessed end would come of this war.

"And then there's Siara," James murmured, his mind returning to the source of his worry. "You of all people should know I could never leave my wife behind. Not while she lay heavy with child."

Ben grunted in understanding since it was the birth of his first son that had led him to abandon his regiment, gather his family, and cross into Canada, thereby securing their freedom. "Nothing sets a man's priorities straight than welcoming his first babe."

James lifted his mug to his lips, not bothering to correct him. It was no business of Ben's, or anyone else's for that matter, to learn that this wouldn't be their first child. The loss of their daughter had been many winters ago, yet the pain of it was still fresh. It was that pain that served to remind James that his fidelity belonged first and foremost to his wife and the children they would create.

"How is your little woman faring, anyhow?"

"She is being tended to by the midwives." James ran his suddenly damp palm down his pant leg. "The babe should be arriving any moment now." And he had left instructions with one of the women to fetch him the minute her labor pains heightened.

"She and the babe will be in my prayers as I for one miss having a skilled and capable medicine woman around."

"Your prayers are appreciated, though it will be a while yet before she is tending to others."

The past few days Siara had been confined to their bed as she waited for the deliverance of their son. He knew she was eager to be out of bed and moving, but James would see to it that she didn't over exert herself.

Ben pulled out a flask from his coat pocket and raised it. "Here's to a swift delivery and easy recovery."

James inclined his head and raised his own mug before taking a long swallow. Ben wasn't the only one who had voiced concern over Siara's impending labor. Many of their friends and neighbors had inquired about her health. Though she wasn't the only medicine woman in their growing community, she was the most sought after and James believed it was largely due to her gentleness and compassion.

They had been lucky to find the settlement when they did two summers ago. The growing violence in

New York had forced them out of their prior community where they had begun to earn a modest living under his altered surname. Brutal attacks on townships throughout the area had escalated, pushing them further west until they had crossed the Niagara River and settled here. It wasn't Africa, but it was home.

Suddenly, a finger tapped on his shoulder and James turned to find one of the midwives wrapped in a thick coat. Fear and anxiety forced him to his feet.

"Siara?"

The older woman nodded. "She's calling for you. It's time."

Siara opened her eyes to find a pair of striking blue eyes staring down at her. She smiled softly.

"James..."

"I'm here, love."

Just as he'd promised, Siara thought as her heart swelled with love. Some days it still felt surreal that the man she had found near death was now truly her husband. Not long after they had parted ways with his men that fateful night in the woods, James had found a clergyman who had been happy to officiate their union.

"As my legal wife, you will now have all the rights to what is mine should anything ever happen to me," he had explained, warmth and affection burning bright in his eyes that night.

But tonight those vivid blue eyes were clouded

with worry. Though he tried to maintain his composure for her sake, she knew just how frantic he was over her impending labor. She touched the side of his scruffy jaw, which was thicker than usual with whiskers.

"You need shave," she teased, wanting to ease some of his worry.

James took her hand and brought it to his lips for a quick kiss. "I don't understand how you can be so calm, love."

Siara gave his hand a gentle but firm squeeze. He returned her reassuring hold with a firm, almost desperate clench of his own.

"You have nothing to fear, James. This time, our babe will live."

She knew that just as she knew in a few hours they would be ushering in a new year and with it a new life with the promise of new beginnings.

"It doesn't change the fact that you will soon be in a great deal of pain."

Siara offered her husband a tender smile just as a cramp seized her lower belly. She gritted her teeth and clenched his hand tighter, waiting for the spasms to subside. James inched closer to her, his brows knitted with worry.

"We are not strangers of pain," she reminded him on a soft pant. "We will manage."

He shut his eyes and nodded stiffly, accepting the truth of her words. The past four years together had been one filled with wonder and exploration. Yet, with their newfound happiness had come unspeakable heartache.

She understood death was a natural course of life, but there was nothing natural about a mother burying her child. Their daughter had come out of her body having never taken her first breath. It was a heartache that hadn't eased and she believed it never would.

Siara rested her hand on her round belly. This time, their babe would live. She had prayed to James' God and to her ancestors that this babe survived and her pleas had been answered. In several of her night visions, she had seen herself holding a babe in her arms while he suckled at her breast. She had also seen a home filled with laughter and children.

Our children.

And this son would be the start of their new family.

Without warning, a heavy pressure settled on her chest. The unexpected discomfort wrenched a gasp from her, bringing James instantly alert. Siara placed her hand over her breasts, but the sudden ache was gone as quickly as it had come.

"What is it, love? Is it the babe?"

She nodded, though she knew it was more than that. She had just lost the woman who had been so much like a mother to her.

Etu.

Siara blinked back her tears, not wanting to alarm her husband, yet she knew in her heart that Etu was now gone from this world. In their four years apart,

Siara had countless night visions of her, but last night had been the first time she'd seen the frail elder in her sick bed. Siara understood that Etu's transition to the spirit world was inevitable. As the birth of their son drew near, Siara also accepted that the new life she would soon bring into this world would be guided by his own guardian—and the spirit of the woman that had once watched over her.

A sharp spasm suddenly seized her belly and Siara grabbed her husband's hand. The pain held her suspended as it traveled around her middle and down her back. The debilitating cramp was immediately followed by another.

There was no more waiting.

"James...the babe," she panted. "He's coming."

James bounded to his feet and went to call out to the midwives. He stood just outside the chamber door as the two women rushed inside.

"James." Siara reached out her hand to him. "Stay with me."

He came back to her side and took her hand. It wasn't customary to have men inside the birthing chamber, but then again, nothing about their union was customary.

"I'm not going anywhere, love." He brought her hand to his lips before gifting her with a brilliant smile. "Are you ready to meet the next James Blakemore?"

Through her discomfort, she managed to laugh. "No one is more ready than I."

AUTHOR'S NOTE

The Battle of Saratoga marked the turning point for the War of Independence (or Revolutionary War) on October 17, 1777, when British General John Burgoyne surrendered to American forces. Before that fateful surrender, Burgoyne waited for assistance from General Sir Henry Clinton, who had promised to send reinforcements to aid Burgoyne in the battle. Aid, however, never arrived. It is not known if Clinton actually sent the soldiers as he, too, was short on officers while he defended the British's control over New York City. Eventually, Burgoyne grew impatient waiting for assistance, forging ahead into battle, which resulted in his surrender.

With the help of the Onyota'aka tribe (known today as the Oneida Indian Nation), the Americans, led by General Horatio Gates, defeated the British in the Battle of Saratoga. The Oneida are one of the five founding nations of the Iroquois Confederacy in the area of upstate New York. The Oneida tribe divided themselves into three clans: the Wolf, Bear, and Turtle. Known as the "First Allies" for their loyalty and support of the Americans during the Revolutionary War, the Oneida were one of the few Indian tribes to ally themselves with the American colonists. More on the Oneida tribe can be read in *Forgotten Allies* by Joseph T. Glatthaar and James Kirby Martin.

In A SWEET SURRENDER, Sergeant James Blake and Siaragowaeh ("Siara") are fictitious characters created for the purposes of this story.

Thanks for reading!

If you enjoyed reading this story, please share with others so they can enjoy it too!

Rate or review the book. Honest reviews are always helpful!

Recommend to your family, friends, and reader groups.

Share with other readers on your favorite social media site.

More Books by Lena Hart

Brides of Cedar Bend series
Something Old
Something New
Something Borrowed
Something Blue

To Be Loved series
First Love
Because You Love Me
Because You Are Mine
Because This Is Forever

The Queen Quartette series
His Flower Queen
His Bedpost Queen
Queen of His Heart
His Diamond Queen

City of Sin spin-off series
B is for Bedpost
The Devil's Bedpost

ABOUT THE AUTHOR

Lena Hart is a Florida native currently living in the Harlem edge of New York City. Though she enjoys reading a variety of romance genres, she mainly writes sensual to steamy contemporary, suspense, and historical romances. When Lena is not busy writing, she's reading, researching, or conferring with her muse. To learn more about Lena and her work, visit LenaHartWrites.com.

IN THE MORNING SUN

Enjoy a special sneak peek!

With the election of 1868 underway, Madeline Asher's mission is clear: educate and enlist the freedmen of Nebraska to vote. After losing the man she loved to war—and a small piece of herself along the way—Madeline leaves her life in Philadelphia behind, determined to reclaim her life's purpose by making a difference in others.

With America's Southern Rebellion at an end, so are the efforts of Union veteran James Blakemore. Tired of the injustices still plaguing the young country, he sets his sights toward his Canadian roots—until fate guides him back to the love he thought he'd lost.

CHAPTER ONE

August, 1868
Southwestern Nebraska

"You're a dangerous woman, Miss Madeline Asher."

Madeline sheathed the small knife into the holder strapped around her wrist. "Better to be a dangerous one then a dead one," she muttered, tugging down the long sleeve of her dress to conceal it.

"What do you plan to do with that gun?"

Madeline ignored her friend and fellow missionary, Sherry Thomas, and proceeded to slip the small Derringer into the holster strapped around her boot ankle.

Teresa Miller snickered. "Someone forgot to tell her the war's over."

Madeline snapped her gaze over at the other

woman. "If you think that, then you're a fool. We're not safe as colored people and we're especially not safe as colored women. Until that day comes, the war will never be over."

Teresa rolled her big, chocolate-brown eyes—an action that left Madeline irritated on enough occasions to make her want to smack the other woman just to see how far back her eyes could roll.

"Don't start up again, Militant Madeline, or I'll have Oliver make you ride outside the stagecoach the rest of the way to Dunesville."

Madeline let her lips stretch into a smile that held no humor or warmth. Their travel from Philadelphia had been long and she about had it with the infuriating woman.

"That's fine by me, Teresa. Your brother keeps better company and it'll save me from having to suffer through your endless chatter."

Teresa sucked in a sharp breath of outrage and as usual, Sherry jumped in to intervene.

"Now, now ladies. It's been a long ride to Nebraska. We're almost to Dunesville and you two need to muster up some of that Philly charm and start getting along. At least through the end of our contracts. Those poor folks out there don't need to suffer through six months of your bickering. Remember, what we're here to do is bigger than your petty squabbles."

Sherry was right.

Madeline couldn't let her irritation with sassy-mouth Teresa Miller turn her into a petty child. She had volunteered to join the missionary so that she could help educate the freedmen of one of the largest Negro communities in Nebraska, not argue sense into Teresa. Now that the old territory had been admitted into the Union as the thirty-seventh state, it was critical that every able-bodied man cast their vote for this election—including the Negro men. And if that meant linking arms with all her sisters to make that happen, Madeline would set aside her differences long enough to do so.

But before Madeline could apologize, Teresa slapped on her travel bonnet.

"Oh, quit your meddling, Saint Sherry." With those crisp words, Teresa stormed out of the room they had all shared for the night.

Madeline turned to Sherry. "I swear that woman exists just to annoy me. I don't know how you put up with her."

"I've known her longer than you."

"Then you really are a saint."

Sherry giggled. "She's really not all that bad."

That remained to be seen. Madeline had only met Sherry last year, after joining the American Missionary Association in Philadelphia, but they had become fast friends—something that almost never happened for Madeline. But where Sherry was pleasant, genuine, and passionate about their cause, Teresa was uppity, arrogant, and praise-seeking.

And what are you?

Wasn't she also here for her own self-serving reasons?

Madeline pushed the uncomfortable thought aside and pinned up the soft coils of her hair atop her head. She took one last look in the mirror, pleased with the way the simple blue gown concealed everything she wanted it to hide, including the remaining bits of fear and anxiety that had travelled with her from Philadelphia.

Her decision to come to Dunesville to teach had not been an impulsive one. The association had been transparent about the dangers the previous instructors had faced by those who had seen their presence as an insult to their bigoted beliefs that Negroes ought to remain uneducated, uninformed, and disinterested in their country's government. She had read about the savagery that had befallen men of color in certain parts of the country who presented any interest in exercising their right to vote, but that had not deterred Madeline from signing on to help with the effort.

As much as she longed for the day when women would be granted those same rights, she couldn't continue to sit idly by, listening to those injustices. It was that same anger and disgust that had led her here, farther west then she had ever been, and she could only hope she could do her part for the freedmen of Dunesville. Maybe then she would find the inner peace that had eluded her for the past two years.

With a wary sigh, Madeline grabbed her small travel bag and started toward the door. "I'll meet you downstairs, Sherry. I need to stop by the postal office before we start off again."

"You're not having breakfast?"

"I'm not particularly hungry this morning." And her nerves were strung too tight for her to try and force down any food. "I won't be long."

Madeline slipped out of the room, her mind already on her next and final task before she, Sherry, and Teresa were dropped off in Dunesville.

Clutching her valise in one hand and the long letter she had written to her sister in another, she made her way down the busy streets and toward the small postal office. It had taken her about three drafts before she had been satisfied with the final letter.

Her final goodbye letter.

Madeline couldn't anticipate how her sister would take the correspondence but if she had to guess, she would assume shock first followed by immense anger. The last thing Madeline wanted to do was anger her only living relative, but the past two years in Philadelphia under her sister's charge had been unbearable. She could no longer stand to be in a city that reminded her so much of what she had lost—nor could she take any more of Elaine's pitying looks. The kind that suggested Madeline would never amount to more than being an unclean and unhappy spinster.

But she was much more than that.

Now that she was of age to access the small inheritance her father had set aside for her, Madeline planned to start a new life for herself elsewhere.

Someplace she could be an asset and truly make a difference—and Dunesville made a great starting place.

Madeline crossed the street and walked down a row of shops. Right before she entered the small postal office, a distinctly tall profile caught her attention. The man stepped out of the bank, his features hidden behind the brim of his hat but there was something oddly familiar about his wide shoulders and smooth, easy stride. He started across the street, his long-legged stride taking him further away from her, yet leaving behind a sense of recognition she couldn't shake.

For a moment, Madeline was held captivated as she was jerked five years into the past...

"I don't want you to go, Jimmy."

His expression softened. "I have to join, Maddie. The victory at Gettysburg was only the beginning. If we want an end to come to this rebellion, the Union needs more men to fight."

"But what of those who have been selected for conscription? The government will have the number of men they need to enlist."

"You've read of what's happening in New York. Those riots are a big setback to our cause and drafting men to fight can't be the only solution. I, for one, will not just sit and wait to be called to fight."

Madeline grabbed his hand and held it tight. "But you can do so much more for our cause here than in any battlefield. You don't need to risk your life!"

"I have a chance to do more than write recruitment

bills and articles. Let me help the Union secure victory against the southern rebels and then you'll see. Soon, everything we've fought hard for will finally be realized."

She swallowed hard, her next words barely a whisper. "And what if you die?"

He brought her hand to his lips then gifted her with his signature smile. "You worry for naught, love. This war is close to coming to an end and you forget. I'm too stubborn to die."

And yet, he had.

When will you stop being so foolish, Maddie? You need to let him go.

The quiet reprimand pulled her out of her stupor and she quickly shook the memory away. Her silly heart and imaginative eyes needed to stop creating visions of him where there were none and accept the fact that her Jimmy was dead. Gone. And after everything she had been through, she should have learned by now that pining for the dead was a waste of time.

Turning on her heels, Madeline pushed open the post office door and stepped inside.

JAMES BLAKEMORE STEPPED out of the bank, fifty dollars richer. It wasn't much but what little he had managed to save from his paltry pension was now rolled up in his boot—and was just enough to see him back home.

He crossed the busy street of the bustling Nebraska city, eager to get started on his long journey east, then north, and finally home. To Canada.

His steps faltered, however, when a strange, warm tingle suddenly moved over him. It was the kind of sensation that came from the penetrating gaze of another. He knew how it felt to have eyes glued on him, and he tended to ignore it.

But this time, it was different.

Turning back, James quickly scanned the crowd for the gawker. There was no one. He caught the glimpse of wide blue skirts disappearing through the doors of the post office. For a moment, the soft sway of the woman's hips brought back a familiarity that made his chest squeeze. James was tempted to go after the lady, but luckily he came to his senses.

It's not her, you blind fool.

With a small shake of his head, James continued down the street. That was the problem of having only one working eye—it kept him from seeing straight. He needed to stop deluding himself. It wasn't her. It couldn't be. His love was far away from here, far away from *him*.

The last he had heard, the woman who should have been his wife had gone to marry some well-to-do miner in Montana. At first, the news had crushed him, but then James had come to accept it. He wasn't the same man he had been when he'd left Philadelphia in hopes of putting an end to one of the greatest atrocities against humanity. He had fought for the Union and emancipation had been declared, but he was now damaged goods.

What did he have to offer a fine woman like Madeline Asher?

"Colonel!"

James turned to find one of the young residents of the new Veteran's House rushing toward him. At the earnestness in the young man's stiff gait, James tensed.

"Philip, what's the matter?"

James waited as the young private stopped to catch his breath. Philip Cooper was a resilient kid, having lost his ability to ever walk straight again during his short stint in the war. But that hadn't stopped him from running the distance he had and James couldn't help but admire that.

"It's Major Anderson, Colonel. He's left the home, but no one's willing to go out and look for him."

James cursed. "Does he have a weapon?"

Philip nodded. "Someone said he stole a chef's knife from the kitchen."

James cursed again. He couldn't blame the other men or paid caregivers for keeping their distance. Major William Anderson could be extremely dangerous. With a knife, he was deadly.

"Do you know which direction he went?"

Philip pointed to the south of them. "I believe he went down to the river. He was shouting something about going to save you."

James pressed his lips in a tight line. When Will began rehashing his time in the prison camp, he was the most unpredictable.

"Thanks, Philip. You did good." He cuffed the

young man on the shoulder. "Now head back to the house and make sure no one else runs off."

"Yes, sir!"

Though the other men in the home weren't as mentally fragile as his friend Will Anderson, it would give the young man something to do while James went to fetch his friend. Turning toward the direction Philip had pointed, James ran down toward the river.

It had taken him quite a bit of convincing before the home would admit his friend. They had thought Will better suited for one of the veteran hospitals back east, but James knew those places were nothing more than dressed up asylums and the conditions would only do more harm than good.

James wouldn't discard his friend in such a place, as many families had done to those who had returned home after the war. Will had no close ties to his family, or anyone willing to take him in, yet a life in an asylum wasn't a fate James could leave his friend to. Not after everything they had been through together. He would see to it that Will lived out the rest of his days in comfort.

As he neared the riverbank, James kept himself vigilant. He couldn't be sure what he would encounter when he got there, but he was careful not to make himself a target.

It didn't take long for James to spot his friend standing in the shallow edge of the river. Will had stripped out of his clothes and was slicing through the water with the long kitchen blade, muttering threats and curses to himself. James jerked off his boots, his hat following next, before he made his way toward his friend.

"Major Anderson! Throw down your weapon. *That's an order.*"

It was a senseless order, since Will appeared more interested in carving answers from the water than following his command. But the goal was to either get Will to drop the blade or distract him enough so James could disarm him of it.

"Those bastards got Jim," Will muttered. "I've got to find him, and then make those bastards pay for what they did."

"No, you don't, Will." James stepped into the water but stopped when Will raised the knife toward him. "It's me, brother. Jim. Your old friend. No one's got me."

Will paused, assessing him with a shrewdness that hadn't been in his bright blue eyes in a while. Then he shook his head wildly.

"No, you're not!" Will began pounding the side of his head. "Jim's dead. *I saw him die.*"

James glanced at the knife in his friend's hand, coming dangerously close to his temple, and his gut twisted. Will could hurt himself—intentionally or not—and with the distance between them, James feared he would be too late to do a damn thing about it.

"Will, look at me. Do I look dead to you? I got this funny looking eye patch but as you can see plain, I'm very much alive."

Will stared at him, recognition flashing across his

flushed face. He lowered the knife and took a tentative step toward him.

"Jim?"

James nodded, keeping his eye on the blade. He held out his hand, urging his friend to hand it to him.

"Yes, brother. It's me. Now why don't you give me that blade and we'll get you back in your uniform."

These days, their uniform consisted of a pair of trousers, one shirt, and a jacket. With the constant fight with the government for adequate pension pay, they were lucky to have those simple provisions.

Will stared down at James' outstretched hand, but instead of taking it, he brought the knife down and slashed it across his palm.

"Liar!"

James jerked back from the intense pain, biting back a vicious curse. Will raised the knife again but this time, James wasn't caught off guard. Grabbing his friend's wrist, he twisted it then slammed his fist against his jaw. Will collapsed with a low grunt. Before he could fall into the river, James caught him and hoisted him over his shoulder.

He carried his unconscious friend to a grassy patch of land and placed him down before he too collapsed beside him. James stared up at the clear sky, waiting for the rapid thudding in his heart to slow. He hated to admit defeat but this struggle between what he wanted for Will versus what was best for him was proving to be a difficult one.

And it was a decision James was starting to realize he wasn't the right person to make.

Will wasn't getting any better and it was time he considered other arrangements for his friend. Before Will seriously hurt himself—or someone else.

As much as he hated it, James knew what he had to do.

Taking in a deep breath, he shut his eyes against the early morning sun, letting the warm rays wash over him. Deep, dark-brown eyes and a pretty smile filled his mind and he smiled back at her. His Maddie.

But the sweet smile he had held constant in his memory turned solemn as he recalled their last night together...

"Maddie, what are you doing here?" James pulled her into his small apartment.

"You're leaving tomorrow, and I know I can't change your mind, so..." She inhaled a shaky breath, her hands clasped before her. "I want to spend tonight with you."

There was an earnestness in her tone that made his heart ache and James reached for her. "Come here, Ladybug." He took her hand in his, and his fingers brushed against something stiff. "What's this?"

Her shy smile only added to his curiosity.

"I had this made for you."

James carefully took the small card from her outstretched hand and turned it over. Staring back at him was her dark, knowing gaze on her smooth, beautiful features. His heart warmed at the sight.

"I have nothing to leave you, love."

She walked up to him and folded her arms around him. "That's all right. Just write to me. Every chance you get."

And he had.

As often as he could, he had sent her countless letters, along with a *carte de visite* when a photographer had been spotted on their camp. Unfortunately, however, her photo and the letters she had written him were now all lost to him, destroyed during the ambush on his regiment.

But James could never forget the love that had shone in his Maddie's eyes that night.

She was the sunlight of his days, the delight of his dreams—and the anchor that had kept his mind from snapping the same way his friend's had.

CHAPTER TWO

"This will be your lodging, Miss Madeline."

She turned away from the tall, well-dressed community leader who would be their host and attendant while she, Sherry, and Teresa were in Dunesville. She surveyed the small, single room cabin and tried not to grimace.

It's only temporary, Madeline reminded herself. She had seen happier living quarters but this one would have to do. And the benefit was that she wouldn't have to share the space.

"Unfortunately, there was some flooding here recently, so it may not be pretty but it's sturdy," Eldridge Duncan said. "Reinforcements were added around the foundation of each place so no need to worry. Only a tornado could knock this place down."

Madeline shared in his short chuckle, though she nervously glanced around the small cabin again.

Since tornadoes were frequent in these parts of the country, it made that possibility an uncomfortable, and frightening, probability.

But Madeline set that worry aside for now. Tomorrow would mark her first day as a teacher and she needed to concentrate on her students, their education, and getting through the next couple of months before the election.

"Thank you, Mr. Duncan. This will do just fine."

Eldridge nodded, a relieved smile breaking across his dark, handsome face.

"We passed by a school on our way here. Is that the one I'll be having my classes in?"

"Indeed, it is," he confirmed. "We were lucky to receive funding to rebuild a new school and church after they were..."

"Burned?" His lips tightened and she gave a small smile of reassurance. "We know all about the vandals that came here and destroyed what you all worked so hard to build, but it hasn't stopped us from coming here and helping."

Another wave of relief flashed across his face. "I'm glad to hear that, Miss Madeline. It was hard finding educated individuals like yourselves to return to Dunesville after that. This community is important to me and my family and we're trying to keep it as safe for our people as we can."

The love and loyalty for what was a thriving community glowed on the man's face. His enthusiasm for the safe haven his family had developed for so many people only added to Madeline's anger that anyone would try to destroy it.

"Well, you don't have to worry about me abandoning you, Mr. Duncan." She offered him a teasing smile. "It's going to take a tornado to sweep me away from here."

He returned her smile and took her hand. "Please, call me Eldridge."

Madeline tensed and stared down at her hand clasped in his. It had been a while since a man had taken her hand that way—with gentleness and affection. But she didn't want his affection.

She wanted nothing from him.

Madeline jerked her hand out of his grasp and his eyes widened in surprise. It was immediately replaced with embarrassment and a sudden awkwardness settled between them.

Regret at her impulsive reaction brought an apology rolling off the tip of her tongue but Madeline swallowed it. What was she to say? That the new Madeline preferred not to be touched, that as much as she liked and respected what he was doing for his community, she didn't want anything other than friendship from him?

The old Madeline wouldn't allow her to be so ill-mannered, so she asked the one thing that mattered.

"What time should I report to the school tomorrow?"

"I believe my mother, Mrs. Ophelia, will discuss that with you all tonight after supper," he said, clasping his hand behind his back. "But everyone is excited for the school term to start again. The children, especially."

"Children?" Madeline frowned. "I specifically requested to teach the adults."

At Eldridge's curious expression, she dropped her gaze down to the button on his coat. Being allowed to teach only the adults had been a big part of her decision to join the mission. Though she may not have been formally trained to teach anyone, she wasn't prepared to deal with children.

"I...I had plans in my curriculum to teach government and politics," Madeline added. "That's where my expertise lay."

"To be frank, I don't really know the details of the teaching assignments, but I don't see why that should present a problem. There will be a noon and evening class schedule for the men to accommodate those who have to work through their noon meal, so you'll have your choice of one."

Madeline released a sigh of relief. Noon or night, it didn't particularly matter to her, so long as it didn't include being near the little ones. Though she knew her preference bordered on ludicrous, she couldn't change how she felt. There were times just the sight of a young child would send her into a panic, or fill her with immense grief. The only way for her to control her reaction was to keep her distance.

After giving her a few more instructions on her accommodations in her temporary residence, Eldridge finally took his leave.

Finally alone in the cabin, Madeline sat down on

the edge of the bed, surprised by its comfort, and took in her surroundings once more. She hadn't imagined her first step toward a new life would come to this—sitting alone in a dim, one-room cabin—but distance from her sister and her past made it worth it.

There was just one person in her past she couldn't seem to let go.

Lifting her travel bag onto the bed, Madeline took out the stack of letters from her suitcase. All of them were from her Jimmy, and every last letter was sacred to her.

Tugging at the thin ribbon around the bundle, she pulled out the top envelop and laid the stack beside her on the bed. It was the first of many letters he had written her and the one she turned to whenever she needed his words to lighten her spirits.

She took out the letter dated five years ago on November fourth, three months after his enlistment and began reading.

My dearest Maddie, I have wanted to write you much sooner as I've missed you more than you can imagine. Though I do not regret my decision to join the Infantry, as I have met with the most honorable and courageous of men, I do regret that we did not wed before my departure. Our last night together is all I can think on. It has firmly bound me to you, as it has bound you to me. You are all that is good and pure of heart, and it is your smile and your passion that sustains me in a place where defeat and despair is rooted in so many. I know in my heart we fight for a great cause, and that this war will soon be over, but I can barely wait for the day when I can truly make you mine. Keep me in your thoughts, my love. I remain always and very truly yours.

Madeline shut her eyes against the sting of tears that burned behind her lids. She knew it was pointless holding on to such mementos, but James Blakemore was the one thing she couldn't seem to leave behind.

Stuffing the letter back into the envelop, Madeline got up from the bed and began settling herself into her new, temporary home.

THE FIRST DAY of class was a massive disappointment.

Madeline sat in the empty classroom, her hands locked together and resting on the desk. She waited over twenty minutes before she accepted the fact that no one was going to show. With a small sigh, she rose to her feet and began to gather her things.

"I was afraid of this, though I had hoped at least a handful would show."

Madeline looked up from her packing to find Mrs. Ophelia Duncan walking into the classroom, her lips pinched with disappointment. Aside from the grays in her neatly-pinned hair, Madeline would never have guessed the head mistress of the school to be in her late fifties. It certainly wasn't evident on her smooth brown face or in her patient brown eyes.

"Perhaps they weren't sure of the time," Madeline offered in response to the empty classroom. She hated to think anyone would pass up the opportunity for a free education.

"I doubt that. We've announced these classes for the past few weeks now, even during the Sunday service. Notices have also been posted around the community." Ophelia sighed.

Madeline could feel the weariness of that small action from where she stood. Last night, she and her missionary mates had shared dinner with Ophelia and from that short time, Madeline had gotten to learn just how much love the Duncan family had for their community.

"Noon may then be a difficult time for them to step away from their work or chores. Perhaps the evening class will be different."

"You're right. Maybe the turn out would be better then. Would it be asking too much if you could lead the evening class? At least until we can figure out a schedule that works for everyone."

"No, it wouldn't be any trouble at all."

That evening, Madeline returned to the school and was relieved to find a few men sitting behind the old desks, waiting for her. It was only a handful—some ranging from young men about her age to a few who could have been old enough to be her father, had he made it to sixty.

She smiled a greeting toward the men only to be met with grim, tired expressions.

"Good evening, class. My name's Madeline Asher and I'm here to teach you reading, writing, and government for the next six months."

Madeline didn't know where her sudden nervousness had come from, but suddenly her hands were clammy and her throat begged for water. She had never taught a group of people before, and the sudden realization that she had absolutely no idea of what she was doing nearly overwhelmed her.

However, the longer she stared out at their expectant faces, the more she realized she needed to get over her nerves and see to her duties. These men had the chance to shape the future of this nation. The laws weren't going to change in the next three months to give the women the right to vote, and with the presidential election barreling down on them, she needed to do the next best thing—equip the freedmen of Dunesville with the knowledge they'd need to cast an informed vote this coming November.

"Miss Madeline? Are you all right?"

Madeline pulled herself out of her daze and offered her class a quick smile. "Yes, thank you. Why don't we go around and introduce ourselves?"

One by one, each man said his name, and told whether he was new to the community. It appeared many of the more enthusiastic men were, in fact, newcomers to Dunesville.

"By show of hands, how many of you know the alphabet?" Madeline asked.

One hand came up.

Madeline bit the inside of her lip. Well, at least now she knew where to start. She took a few minutes to explain what the alphabet was and why it was important to learn. Some of the men listened to her intently and with genuine interest. A few others, however, were not as invested. She tried to ignore that unfortunate fact, yet the more cynical their expressions turned, the more she began to lose her confidence—and her resolve.

So she decided to tackle the most stubborn bull of the group head on.

"Mr. Barnes, what would you like to learn to write first?"

Surprise flashed in the older man's dark eyes before it was replaced with sharp skepticism. "Miss Madeline, I appreciate all that you're trying to do here, but truthfully, I see no point to it. These white folks don't give a lick about our vote. They gon' put whoever the hell they want in that big ole' house and there ain't nothing we can do about that."

Madeline glanced around the room as some of the men murmured in agreement. She could understand their frustration, especially with news of the Black Codes taking root and spreading across the South. Those unsanctioned laws made it difficult for Negro men and women to function as equal citizens of the country.

But Madeline couldn't let the attitude of one influence the others. Not when there was so much at stake.

"Mr. Barnes, we can only make a difference if we take a stand and let our voices be heard. I'm trying to give you the tools you need to march to that voting poll and cast your ballot for the candidate you believe has an interest in your rights as an American citizen."

Mr. Barnes scoffed and settled back in his seat, his thick arms folded across his wide chest. "Darling, I'm too old and too tired to believe in those fairytales you spinning. You can stop with all that voting mess. I'm not about to get lynched for putting down a name on a piece of paper for some white man who's feeding us nothing but lies."

He received more murmurs and nods of approval and Madeline's heart sank. They were losing faith in the system and her class without really giving it a chance.

"Think about this, Mr. Barnes. If the election weren't so important, there wouldn't be people out there right now trying to keep you out of it. As a newly freed man in this nation, you can't let your fear or frustration keep you from practicing your constitutional right. At the very least, don't let what all those brave soldiers fought for become a lost cause."

"If you ask me, it's already a lost cause. They killed the only white man in power who seemed to be on our side. They already got us back in chains. And it's a real shame, because this time, a lot of us just can't see it."

At Mr. Barnes words, many of the other men grew vocal in their agreement. But it was the indifferent callousness of what he said that struck her—and made her see red.

It's already a lost cause?

How could he say that? With all that she had lost —all that she and so many others had given up—she couldn't accept that it had all been for nothing.

With short, careful steps, Madeline went to stand in front of the desk Mr. Barnes sat behind. She dragged the desk back and slid it off to the side.

"If that's how you feel, Mr. Barnes, then you are free to leave my classroom." Madeline turned to the other men in the room. "All of you are. I won't waste my time with a bunch who cares nothing about their future, much less the future of their children. I particularly won't waste my time with an ignorant, selfish bunch that can't appreciate the opportunity they've been given."

A few hung their heads low, but Mr. Barnes continued to glare defiantly back at her. She knew there were still some who followed his belief and total disregard for the American democratic system. Though she could understand their apprehension, their fear, she couldn't tolerate their disregard of those who had fought and died for them to have this moment.

"You have a chance here, gentlemen, to honor your country and those who gave their lives so you could have this right. You also have an opportunity to honor your mothers, sisters, and daughters and be their champions for change. Those women look to you to be their voice in a country that says they can't have one, simply because they are women—a decree passed on by men brought into this world by women. *That*, gentlemen, is the true shame."

The silence in the room was louder than a cannon blast—and just as unnerving.

Madeline's heart thudded in her chest as she continued to glare down at a quiet Mr. Barnes. She felt the eyes of the other men on her but kept her gaze on the one stubborn bull who had started her on her tirade.

"So, Mr. Barnes, are you going to leave here and give those who mean to terrorize and oppress us exactly what they want? Or will you remain here with me and let me help you serve and honor what this country stands for?"

The older man slowly rose to his feet and Madeline took a step back, a sinking sense of failure crawling up her spine. But to her surprise, Mr. Barnes grabbed the desk she had set aside and slid it back to its original place. He fell into his seat.

"My name."

Madeline cocked her head to the side. "Excuse me?"

"You asked what I wanted to learn to write first." Mr. Barnes cleared his throat. "I want to write my name."

CHAPTER THREE

"That looks pretty bad, Jim. You sure you want to ride out tonight?"

James glanced down at his bandaged hand and shrugged. Considering the various injuries he had endured since his enlistment, a knife to the hand amounted to nothing more than an inconvenience.

"I still got one good eye and one good hand. I'll live."

Clayton Palmer snorted. "You always managed to see the bright side of things."

James placed his signature on the last of the government documents and handed them to his attorney and fellow Union vet.

"Well, I believe happier things come when we keep our eyes locked toward the sun." That way, his shadows would always stay behind him. "Besides,

I'm already a day behind on my journey. The sooner I'm on my way, the better."

Clay sighed. "I wish you would reconsider. There's still so much work to be done."

"I've done all that I can do, Clay. I've signed more petitions then I can remember and sat in more assembly meetings than I can stomach. Perhaps when the bureaucrats in Washington are ready to enforce half of the promises they've made to their countrymen, to the men who fought for them, then perhaps I'll consider continuing the good fight. Until then...my work here's done."

The solemn, half-hearted smile on Clay's face was all the acknowledgement James needed. They both knew he had a point. They may not agree on the level of change that needed to take place, but they both agreed that it wasn't happening soon enough.

"In the short time I've known you, Jim, I always pegged you as a man with strong beliefs, but I've always wanted to know why..."

"Why, what?"

"Why fight? Why risk your life for a country you had no stake in? You clearly don't plan to stay, so why?"

The corner of James's lips lifted into a half smile. He was not offended by the question because he had asked himself that very thing when times had been beyond bleak, and when those times had appeared damn-near hopeless. There were countless reasons, little of which having to do with him being in love with a colored woman and a lot to do with the fact that America was part of his roots.

"I may not be American born but my great-grandmother was part African and part Iroquois," James confessed. "Her tribe fought with the Americans during the revolution. I like to think I'm finishing that fight for *all* Americans to be free."

In many ways, his ancestry made him as American as any man here, and a land that embodied the spirit of freedom and new life shouldn't continue to stain its legacy with the enslavement of people.

If the knowledge that he was the descendent of a colored woman surprised Clay, his friend didn't show it. His fair skin, dark-brown wavy hair, and light green eyes hid that part of his heritage, allowing him to move about this country as freely as any full-blooded white man. But in the eight years James had lived in this country, he knew that the knowledge of his full ancestry would put an end to those privileges he was granted.

"Well, we're going to miss you around here," Clay said, apparently choosing to ignore that bit of damning information. "Fighting the good fight."

"It certainly was a fight well fought," James muttered.

And if he were honest with himself, James was going to miss it here, too. More specifically, he was going to miss the friends he had made, the places he'd been, and the ones he had yet to see. He had always had a strange pull to this country. Maybe it was the tales his father had told him of the first James

Blakemore. Their family's original patriarch had fought fearlessly for the British during the birth of this young nation—until he had met the woman that he would choose to give it all up for, just so they could be together.

That had once been a dream of his as well—to return to his home in Canada with the woman he loved. But fate had seen to it that his Maddie found love and happiness with another. As much as James resented the thought of her with another man, he couldn't begrudge her the one thing he had always wanted for her.

Happiness.

James rose to his feet, ignoring the unrelenting tightness that always seem to invade his chest whenever he thought of their broken future. As much as he would miss this great land, there was nothing left for him here.

"Well, I better be off. It's high-time my family saw my charming face again, not to mention the new nieces and nephews I have yet to meet. You know where to contact me, if you need me."

Clay stuffed the documents giving him power-of-attorney over James' U.S. assets into a file before he too got to his feet. "Everything I need is all in there. And not to worry about Anderson. Until I hear back from his kin, I'll be sure he gets his pension, and whatever else he needs at the home."

James nodded. Guilt over leaving Will behind, before he had a chance to get in touch with his half-sister, almost made him second guess his decision to leave. His friend was sick, the kind of sick no doctor could fix. James could only hope that Will's sister did right by him and used his pension to see to his comfort.

"Write to me if you run into any issues."

Clay took his hand and gave it a firm shake. "Of course. Safe travels, Jim."

With a quick tip of his hat, James left Clay's law office and headed toward the post office. He had one last errand to run before he started on his long journey home.

He entered the small office and went straight to the front counter. It was hard to miss the gaping stare of the young clerk. James ignored him. There were times he managed to forget about the patch covering his right eye, forget the scars that traced a jagged path down the side of his face.

Today, however, wasn't one of those times.

"I need these three letters postmarked today." James handed the older clerk behind the desk the envelopes, trying his damnedest to ignore the fascinated gaze of the young man off to the side. He hated being gawked at. Oftentimes, people stared long enough to satisfy their curiosity, but they eventually had the damn decency to look away.

"Where is this one going?" The old man's eyeglasses sat perched on the bridge of his nose as he squinted down at one of the letters in his hand.

"Canada," James replied.

The old man grunted, then made a notation on the envelope. Without looking up, the clerk slid a short form across the counter toward him. "I'm gonna need some more information from you, sir. Derrick, that mail ain't gonna sort itself."

James glanced over at Derrick as he took the form. The young man remained standing there, a stack of mail clutched in his hands and his wide-eyed gaze held transfixed on his eye patch.

With a sigh of exasperation, James shifted until he was standing directly in front of the young mail clerk. Leaning against the counter, James got as close as he could and flipped open his eye patch.

"Here's a closer look."

The blood drained from Derrick's face and to his surprise, the boy collapsed were he stood. James released the eye patch and it fell back into place. Leaning over the counter, he peered down at the unconscious boy, mail littered all over him.

"Well, hell."

The old man sucked at his teeth and shook his head. "He's always had a weak stomach. Didn't figure him a fainter too."

"Your son?"

"Nope. My late sister's boy, so I guess I got to claim him." The man moved to grab the boy's feet. "Help me with him, would ya?"

James came around the counter and grabbed Derrick's shoulders. Together, they moved the boy's motionless body to a nearby seat. The man stood back with a grunt then turned and studied him closely.

"I'm guessing you lost that eye in the war?"

James gave a curt nod. Though he hadn't lost it fighting in battle, the result had been just the same. He wondered just how good a look the man had gotten at the damaged, hollowed socket. The older clerk hadn't flinched when he'd exposed the scarred remains of his right eye socket. James could only assume he hadn't gotten that good a look because he knew just how grotesque the sight was. There were days where he avoided his own reflection.

"Lost a brother in that damn war." The clerk shook his head with pity. "I reckon, though, he'd rather be dead then a—"

"Cripple?" James finished for him.

The man's face flushed with embarrassment. James ignored the man's obvious discomfort. That was the problem with some westerners, he had come to realize. They always had an opinion and never knew when to keep it to themselves.

"I knew a few men like that, too vain to live a life with a mutilated face," James said evenly. "But if you ask me, nothing beats death. Not even vanity."

Derrick began to stir in his seat. "Uncle Aaron…?"

The old clerk went to tend to his nephew, clearly grateful for the distraction.

James started back around the other side of the counter when he realized he was crushing a letter beneath his boot. He snatched it up and started to toss it back on the counter when the handwriting caught his attention. It was the way the letters scrolled neat and elegantly across the front of the envelope that drew him.

He clutched the envelope in his hands as he carefully read the name of the sender. Then he re-read it again, not wanting to put his trust in fate again—or allow himself to believe in miracles.

Yet the name on the envelope didn't disappear...
Madeline Asher.

He knew that handwriting well. With every letter that had made its way to him during the darkest moments of his hell, he had studied her writing, memorized her words. This was her name, her handwriting, and—he brought the letter to his nose—her scent.

James whipped around to the clerk and his nephew. The look on their faces made him question his own sanity. Maybe the sweet, delicate smell he remembered was all in his head, but he didn't care. He knew with every fiber in his being that this was her.

And he needed to find her.

"The woman who brought this in, when was she here?"

The two men stared blankly at him. James cursed.

"*When*, damn it?"

Aaron snapped out of his stupor. "I don't rightly know. We had a lot of traffic yesterday and today..."

"This patron would have been hard to miss. She's about yay high." James levelled his hand up to the center of his chest. "She has big, chestnut brown eyes and smooth, amber-brown skin. The color of sweet butterscotch." James shut his eye briefly, wanting to imprint the memory of her in his mind. "She has the sweetest smile and the softest laugh…"

"I'm starting to realize, Mr. James Blakemore that you have this perverse need to tease me."

"I can't seem to help myself, Miss Asher. It must be the fire in your eyes that I find irresistible."

She laughed again and shook her head. "You are as peculiar as you are vexing."

He smiled down at her, enchanted by the sweet sound of her laugh. "I assure you, I'm as ordinary as they come. But a passionate lady deserves an impassioned suitor."

"Am I to presume that suitor to be you?"

"Well, love, you have managed all three of the impossible."

Her eyes widened at the endearment, but she didn't shy away. "And what is that?"

Further emboldened, James took her hand and kissed her wrist. "You have aroused my mind, inflamed my senses, and corrupted my thoughts."

He opened his eye again, having lost himself in that short glimpse into the past—to his initial courtship of the most captivating and easily goaded woman he had ever met. James caught the shared look between the two clerks and a bit of warmth crawled up his cheeks.

But he refused to lose his resolve.

"I need to find her. Now, do you know where she is?"

"No," Aaron said. "I don't remember a woman by that…colorful description coming in here."

"You have her letter right here," James snapped. "She came in here sometime today. Now think!" He turned to the younger clerk. "What day were those letters you were sorting postmarked?"

Derrick's already pale face lost what little remaining color it had. "Th-th-they were collected yesterday."

"So you saw her?"

The young man's eyes darted from him to his uncle. "Maybe... I-I don't remember. I think so."

James sighed and bit back a curse. He was getting nowhere but needed a starting place if he was going to find her in this busy town.

"Do you remember a colored woman stopping in here? Perhaps one you'd never seen before?" The boy opened his mouth, indecision plain on his face. "Think long and hard before you answer, Derrick."

Something in his tone must have convinced him, because the boy shut his eyes and James watched as the pupils moved rapidly behind his eyelids. Then suddenly, they sprang open.

"I remember!"

James' gut clenched in anticipation.

"She came in very early. I believe you were in the back, Uncle Aaron."

"Do you know where she's staying?"

"No, sir. But I heard of some colored missionaries staying at Patty's Saloon. She could have been traveling with them."

"Traveling?"

"Y-yes. She asked about renting a box for her

letters. Asked about our schedule, too, so she knew what times to travel into town."

"Did she say when she would be back?"

The young man shook his head vehemently.

James took a step forward. He was so close! "Are you certain?"

"He said he doesn't know," Aaron interjected. "Now, I think it's about time you finish your business here, mister, and be on your way."

James snapped his gaze over to the older man.

Maddie is my business.

But he kept the sharp retort behind his teeth. At least now, he had a starting place.

And by the following night, he finally had a destination.

Dunesville.

CHAPTER FOUR

"I heard you gave your class a proper and thorough set down last night, Maddie."

Madeline swung her gaze over at Sherry, embarrassment warming her cheeks as she thought about her rant to a room full of grown men.

"I wouldn't call it a set down..." Madeline began.

"Then what would you call it?"

More like a meltdown.

When she'd had a moment to calm down, Madeline realized how improper her behavior had been. Though the men had stayed until the end, including Mr. Barnes, and had showed a little more interest in her teaching, Madeline wouldn't be surprised if none of them showed today. Why would they?

Upon further reflection, she had a chance to think about the men's arguments. As colored men, they faced constant humiliation and degradation from the hands of their counterparts. The last thing they wanted was an "uppity" colored woman talking down to them. It certainly was the last thing they needed.

"Well, whatever you call it," Sherry said, "it seemed to work. It's all anyone can talk about today."

"Wonderful," Madeline muttered. "I'm glad I'm the source of everyone's afternoon gossip."

Sherry laughed. "And this morning. I had breakfast with the Duncans and even they were talking about it."

Madeline groaned. She typically chose to skip her morning meal, and was glad for it. Now she would have to find time to explain her behavior to Ophelia.

"Well, enjoy this now," Madeline said. "Because it'll be the last. I plan to apologize to the men tonight for my behavior. At least to whoever decides to show up…"

Sherry shrugged. "From what I hear, there's nothing for you to apologize for, Maddie. The Duncans admired what you did. You're a teacher now, a mentor to your pupils, and sometimes that means ruling with an iron fist."

Madeline frowned. "These are grown men we're talking about, not children. How will I expect to gain their respect if I go around talking down to them and making them feel low?"

Sherry shook her head. "Take it from someone who teaches children, being firm-handed doesn't mean you're talking down to them. You think I go around coddling my kids? No. I praise them often when they have earned it, and reprimand them when they misbehave or challenge my authority. Don't go undoing what you've done, Maddie. You have their attention and respect now. Use that to continue pushing them."

Though Madeline wanted to be as optimistic as Sherry, she couldn't help feeling as if she had already set a negative precedent and she had a lot of work ahead of her if she was going to convince any of them to return to her class.

Later that evening, Madeline realized she had gotten it all wrong. She entered the classroom and her mouth fell open.

The room was packed.

Not only did it include new male faces, there were also some women in attendance. Madeline surveyed the room of black and brown faces—some behind desks, others on the floor—all looking to her with interest and an excitement she hadn't seen before. There were maybe about twenty to twenty-five people in the small classroom and they were all ready to learn.

"If it's okay with you, Miss Madeline, some of us would also like to learn to write our names."

"And maybe read what's in those books you carry around," another called out.

"Yeah, I'd like to learn to read a few pages myself," someone else shouted from the back.

Madeline beamed at all of them, her heart swelling with wonder and another emotion she couldn't name.

"Of course it's all right," she said. "I just hope some of you are comfortable on the ground like that. This class runs for about an hour."

"Yup, Miss Madeline. We're all good down here," someone from the ground called out. "Just as long as the ground is the hardest thing my backside is going to suffer in your class."

Everyone laughed and Madeline couldn't help but join in their amusement.

"I promise you, it is," she assured them. "Now, shall we get started?"

It was high noon when James rode into Dunesville.

If he had thought finding Madeline in the private community would come easy, he learned swiftly just how private and guarded the people of Dunesville really were.

He'd been there less than an hour, and yet all his questions about Madeline Asher had been met with silence and blank stares.

But James knew she was here. He felt it in his gut. Nothing, not even the residents' wariness of him, would stop him from searching for her.

He made his way to the church, hoping he would find better luck there. The mail clerk had mention something about her being part of a missionary group. If he was lucky, his search would end there.

James drew his horse alongside the large white building and jumped off. He tethered it to a nearby tree, never taking his attention off of the newly but poorly assembled building. After helping construct over a dozen veteran homes these past two years, James could spot poor handiwork and lazy construction from just one glance.

As he neared the church, a loud crash came from inside, followed by a heavy grunt. James rushed inside to find a short, balding man dressed in a long, black robe and starched white neck collar. The man appeared to be about fifty, yet he was attempting to lift a pew that had sunken into the floor boards on his own.

Without a word, James went to the other end of the pew. The reverend glanced up at him, perspiration glistening above his dark brows and brown face, and his eyeglasses were dangerously close to sliding off of his nose.

James grabbed the bottom of the pew. "On three."

He started counting and on three, they managed to lift the heavy bench enough to slide it out of its trench. The reverend straightened and adjusted his robe.

The man gave him a quick once over, his narrowed gaze not hiding his obvious suspicion. A sinking feeling settled in James' gut when he realized his hope for answers would not be found here either.

"You the carpenter from town?"

James nodded stiffly. It wasn't a complete lie since he'd spent the last three months there working on the new veteran home. That had to count.

The reverend's lips pursed with disapproval.

"What took you so long, then? Oliver said he sent for you hours ago."

James jerked at the unexpected question. He was just about to tell the man that he was mistaken until he realized his advantage. Though, James didn't like the idea of deceiving a man of God, he had to know if what he felt in his gut was right.

"Sorry about that, Reverend," James began. "I was held up on another job."

The reverend grunted. "You could have sent word. I told them the floors have been groaning for weeks now. Had you been here sooner, I wouldn't be in this predicament."

"Again, my apologies." James held out his hand. "Lieutenant Colonel James Blakemore, at your service, sir."

The reverend shook his hand, and James knew the title had impressed him as he had intended it to. Whatever he needed to do to gain the man's trust...

"Reverend George Lincoln. Named after our two great presidents," the man said proudly. "But everyone calls me Reverend Linc. You a Union soldier, James?"

"Yes, sir. Served in the one-hundred and fifth Infantry regiment." James glanced back down at the collapsed floor. "I didn't have time to get the details from my boss, but I'm guessing you need the floor beds secured?"

"Ha! That's just the beginning."

The reverend proceeded to list all the repairs

around the church that needed work. And it was quite a list.

"Do you have all the supplies for these tasks?" James asked.

The reverend shrugged. "I might. Everything during and after the construction was stored in the cellar. You're welcome to take a look to see what else we might need."

James inclined his head. "Lead the way."

Reverend Linc led him outside of the church and around the back. It was then he decided to broach the subject.

"I heard there were some missionaries that arrived here the other day," James began in what he hoped was a casual tone. "Are they all residing here at the church?"

"Oh, no. Those ladies are staying in the red cabins."

James' heart leapt with anticipation. She was here.

"If you ask me," Reverend Linc continued, "they're better off there too. Those small shacks are a far sight better than this building, with its weak walls and floors."

"The church looks new. Why the feeble construction?"

"Why you think? One of those vagabonds in town burnt down our first building. I reckon they figured it'll come down again so why bother building something sturdy?"

James frowned. "Have you taken this up with the sheriff?"

The reverend turned and gave him an incredulous look. "I can't be too certain he wasn't the one who lit the fire." Suddenly, as if realizing he'd said too much, Reverend Linc pursed his lips and continued toward the tall cellar door.

From the wary glance the reverend had shot him right before he had turned away, James could only guess the vandals had been white men. Although he resented the idea of someone of the law neglecting to protect their citizens, James wasn't exactly surprised by it. Before and since the war, he had the misfortune of meeting extremely hateful, bigoted men. As much as James sympathized with the small community's unfortunate situation, he needed to focus on the real reason he was there—before the reverend did like everyone else in the community and completely shut him out.

"So about those cabins, are you sure they're secure? If they're close by, maybe I can drop by and take a look at them."

Reverend Linc unlatched the door and pulled it open with a hard tug. "I believe they're about two, three miles west of here, but it could—Hey! Where you off to?"

James didn't stop in his tracks when he called back. "Sorry, Reverend. I just realized I'm late for an appointment."

About three years too late.

James got to his horse and started off toward the direction the reverend had mentioned. In a mad gallop, he made it to the row of small, red cabins in record time. It was a little after noon yet the area appeared desolate. For a moment, James wondered if the reverend had gotten their location mistaken until he saw a young woman leaving from one of the cabins. He swung his horse in her direction and rushed toward her.

The woman froze, her dark eyes saucers as she clutched an armful of books to her chest. James immediately dismounted and pulled off his hat.

"Sorry, Miss. I don't mean to bother you. I'm looking for Maddie—Madeline Asher. Can you point me to her cabin?"

The woman glanced toward his eyepatch, and then continued staring at him. For a moment, James wondered if she too would ignore him as the others had. He held on to his waning patience.

"Reverend Linc sent me," James lied.

Well, it's not a complete lie.

"The cabin on the end is where Maddie stays," the woman finally said. "But she might still be at the school."

School?

James simply inclined his head. With one final look in his direction, she continued down the path. He led his horse toward the last cabin down the row, his heart thudding in his chest.

Suddenly, he found himself torn between his anticipation to see her and his fear of how she would react when she saw him. As much as he wanted to lay his sights on her, to touch and hold her, there was a part of him that was afraid that she wouldn't be as eager to see him.

Five years was a long time since they'd laid eyes on each other. He wasn't the same man she'd known before the war. He no longer looked the same. With his damaged face, what if she found him repulsive? Frightening?

What if she had moved on from him?

James tethered his horse nearby and walked up to the cabin. Like he had done many times before, especially during the pits of battle, he shoved his fears and uncertainty deep inside himself. Fate—and perhaps even God—had brought him this far.

There was no turning back now.

MADELINE WAS PLEASED with yet another successful day with her students.

The men and women of Dunesville were more eager about their education than she had realized— or had given them credit for. Because the previous evening's class had been overcrowded, she had managed to convince those who could spare the time to attend the mid-day classes, saving the evening ones for those who needed it the most.

Today, she had gotten a decent turnout with a group that was just as eager about the upcoming classes and the thought filled Madeline with a quiet happiness and excitement.

As she made her way back to her cabin, the high afternoon sun beat down on her, adding to her lightheadedness and fatigue from the long walk from the school. She made a mental note to start eating something in the mornings before class, at least until the end of this sweltering summer, or else she wouldn't have the stamina to teach anyone anything.

Madeline continued toward her small cabin, making another mental note to start carrying a hat with her to ward off the harsh sun. By the time she made it through the door of her cabin, she couldn't think of anything more heavenly than the pitcher of cool water inside.

Madeline dropped her bag of books on the ground and rushed to the pantry. She reached for the pitcher and mug until she realized they both weren't where she had left them.

She froze.

The hairs on the back of her neck stood on end, and she could sense with every fiber in her being that she wasn't alone. Panic swelled inside her but she swiftly suppressed it. She wasn't the same helpless Maddie she had been two years ago. She began to slowly slide the knife out of her wrist holster, wishing she had her pistol in the same easy reach.

Once she had the knife from its sheath, Madeline whirled around to face her intruder.

Instead, she came face to face with a ghost.

The bottom dropped from her stomach, along with the knife from her hand. She had dreamed of that moss-green gaze and sensual lips that had stretched into a wicked smile whenever he had fancied a kiss from her.

Madeline shook her head.

No, this can't be him.

The Jimmy she knew was dead and her mind was playing tricks on her. This strange man who bore the ravages of violence on one side of his face was just a larger, coarse, and damaged imitation of the man she had once known. He was here to hurt her and like before, she would be too weak, too stupid, to stop him.

Yet, with just a few simple words—words spoken in the same deep, richly smooth voice she remembered so well—the man managed to strip away the last of her defenses.

"I've missed you, Ladybug."

Madeline gaped at him. Suddenly, something strange moved over her and the blood drained from her head.

To her immense horror, she fainted.

∼

Continue James and Maddie's story in IN THE MORNING SUN.

Made in the USA
Middletown, DE
10 March 2018